MORE FROM MIKE KNOX

Vivien's Rain: My Daughter's Battle with Epilepsy

Straight Fish, A Novel of Life Behind Bars:
A Correctional Officer's Story

MORE FROM
THE SAGER GROUP

The Swamp: Deceit and Corruption in the CIA
An Elizabeth Petrov Thriller (Book 1)
by Jeff Grant

Eat Wheaties: A Novel
by Michael Kun

#MeAsWell: A Novel
by Peter Mehlman

Death Came Swiftly: Novel About the Tay Bridge Disaster of 1879
by Bill Abrams

High Tolerance: A Novel of Sex, Race, Celebrity, Murder ... and
Marijuana by Mike Sager

Miss Havilland: A Novel
by Gay Daly

The Orphan's Daughter: A Novel
by Jan Cherubin

Lifeboat No. 8: Surviving the Titanic
by Elizabeth Kaye

Into the River of Angels: A Novel
by George R. Wolfe

Goodbye, Sweetberry Park: A Novel of City Life,
Creeping Gentrification and Flesh-eating Snakes
by Josh Green

See our entire library at TheSagerGroup.net

A NOVEL

ISLA VISTA HALLOWEEN

A NOVEL OF COLLEGE LOVE, ANGSTY ROAD TRIPS AND MEETING JESUS CHRIST

MIKE KNOX

Isla Vista Halloween: A Novel of College Love, Angsty Road Trips and Meeting Jesus Christ
Copyright © 2025 Mike Knox
All rights reserved.

No part of this publication may be reproduced, stored in a retrieval system, or transmitted, in any form or by any means, electronic, mechanical, photocopying, recording, or otherwise, without the prior written permission of the publisher.

Published in the United States of America.

Cover and interior designed by Siori Kitajima, PatternBased.com

Cataloging-in-publication data for this book is available from the Library of Congress

ISBN-13
eBook: 978-1-958861-61-5
Paperback: 978-1-958861-62-2

Published by The Sager Group LLC
(TheSagerGroup.net)

A NOVEL

ISLA VISTA HALLOWEEN

MIKE KNOX

Once in a while you get shown the light in the strangest
of places if you look at it right.

—Robert Hunter

CONTENTS

CHAPTER 1 1

CHAPTER 2 9

CHAPTER 3 25

CHAPTER 4 37

CHAPTER 5 43

CHAPTER 6 47

CHAPTER 7 55

CHAPTER 8 59

CHAPTER 9 63

CHAPTER 10 67

CHAPTER 11 73

CHAPTER 12 77

CHAPTER 13 81

CHAPTER 14 87

CHAPTER 15 97

CHAPTER 16 105

CHAPTER 17 111

CHAPTER 18 123

About the Author 137

About the Publisher 138

CHAPTER 1

Scarlet and I had been in love, but lately I hadn't heard from her. She had moved home to New Hampshire and wasn't returning my calls. I still had a coffee mug with her lipstick stain on it in my cupboard. It was summer now in Isla Vista. I hadn't seen her in six months.

I arrived at Burbank Airport early. The sun was bright. I went inside for a drink at the lounge. I spotted Cassidy. She looked good. We sat down after hugging each other like long lost friends.

"Jack, you look awful," she said.

"Thanks."

"What did you drink last night?" she asked.

"Everything."

"Did you miss me?"

"A little."

She smiled. "Well, I missed you too."

"Have you got any aspirin?" I asked.

"Yeah, somewhere in my bag." Cassidy dumped her purse on the table and fumbled through it. She had been Scarlet's college roommate in Isla Vista. She'd gotten her nose pierced with a silver hoop and had stopped shaving her legs. She said she liked the way they sparkled in the sunshine. Her hair was curly blonde. She had it in a hat because she was trying to grow dreadlocks. She was wearing a tie-dye shirt and ripped jean shorts with leather sandals.

Anna arrived dressed in a business suit. She was holding a laptop. She had also lived with Scarlet in Isla Vista. It scared me to think that she had her life together before I did.

"Well, if it isn't Jack Miller!" she said. "You look horrible."

"I've been drunk for three days," I said.

"Good for you."

I leaned over the table and hugged her.

"Well, enough about you, how do you like my hair?"

"It's nice," I said.

"I just got it cut. What do you think Cassidy, too short?"

"It's fine," I said.

"Oh, you don't really care," said Anna, brushing me off. "Tell me what you think, Cassidy."

"I like it," said Cassidy, nodding like a child.

"Me too," said Anna, agreeing with her. "So, have you talked to Scarlet?"

"No," I said. "I just bought my ticket and figured I'd surprise her."

"I already told her you were coming. How'd you afford your ticket anyway?"

"I sold my car."

"You must really love her."

"Don't tell her I sold it."

"Why not?" asked Cassidy.

"'Cause she'll get mad and I don't need that."

"But why?"

"Just do me a favor and promise me that you won't say anything?"

"I promise."

"Thank you."

"What have you been up to?" asked Anna.

"Not much," I said, tilting my drink. "What about you?"

"I just got back from Italy two days ago, and before that I was in France. I think I want to go back there and go to school next year. I need to learn French. How was your trip, Cassidy?"

"It was a lot of fun."

"Where did you go?" I asked.

"I went to a semester at sea in the Mediterranean."

"Let's go find our flight," said Anna.

We made our way through the metal detectors. Prohibited items were: axes, bats, bows, brass knuckles, whips, cattle prods, crossbars, dynamite, hammers, hockey sticks, knives, guns, mace, nunchucks, razors, scissors, drills, rifles, swords, spears, stun guns, throwing stars, and toy weapons.

We went through the line quickly and found our flight. I saw Eddie Van Halen leaning against a wall. I wanted to tell him I knew him—that he used to drive down my street on San Pasqual in Pasadena. I used to stand out in front of my house and watch him race his 1940s hot rod. My mother would tell me that he was the devil because of the music he played so I would yell, "Here comes the devil!"

I kept it to myself and never said a word to the girls. After all, who would believe me?

Our plane arrived and we boarded. I found my seat and sat down. I got lucky. No one was sitting next to me.

The flight attendants appeared, pushing carts down the aisles, smiling.

I had a turkey sandwich, chocolate chip cookie, and buttered sourdough bread. I washed it all down with a cold beer and felt that it was one of the best meals I'd ever had. I put the trash on the empty seat next to me and folded up the tray.

Cassidy was standing over me when I woke up. "Get up," she said. "We're here."

"Are we in Dallas?" I asked, still half asleep.

"No stupid, we're in Boston."

"Well, let's go," I said, with a little excitement. I stretched for a second and then followed Cassidy off the plane.

My eyes scanned the crowd for Scarlet. The crowd separated. Scarlet was standing alone. She had never looked so good. I hesitated to go to her. I didn't want to look like I was in love with her.

I hugged Delilah first and then shook hands with her husband Sam. They had been my college roommates in Isla Vista. Delilah was naturally pretty with long brown hair. Sam was a speed freak who talked too fast, but he was loyal. Sam was lucky to have Delilah for his wife.

Time stood still when I turned and caught Scarlet waiting for me. All the old memories came flooding back. I grabbed her and told myself never to let go. I had thought my feelings for her were going to be different, but nothing had changed. I loved her. Her tan skin felt smoother than I had remembered. I ran my hands from her shoulders down to her wrists and squeezed her just enough to assure myself that she was real. My head was resting on her blonde hair that smelled like vanilla. I loved every detail of her. I wanted to tell her I loved her, but I didn't. I was speechless.

I took a step back, lost in her blue eyes. The loneliness from a long college break had been lifted. I felt the freedom of my youth.

"Let's get a drink," I said to the others.

"We've got to find my car," said Scarlet.

"It's in the middle of nowhere," said Delilah.

Scarlet counted heads. "I don't know how we're going to fit everything in my Jeep."

"We'll figure it out," I assured her.

We stuffed Scarlet's Jeep until there was no more room, then piled the rest on the roof. Sam and I used our shoelaces to tie down the bags.

"I lost my wallet at the hotel," said Scarlet. "I'll have to lie to my dad about that."

"My car broke down in Boston," Sam added. "I've got to pick it up tomorrow and make sure those bastards don't screw me."

"So," said Scarlet. "We're going to stop off at the hotel and see if they found my wallet."

"How much was in it?" asked Anna.

"A lot. My dad's going to kill me."

We stopped off at the hotel and waited in the parking lot while Scarlet went inside. I was praying she would find it, but she didn't.

"It's not there," she whined. The sun was dipping under the horizon. We got back on the highway. Scarlet was still wearing the poison ring I had given her for her nineteenth birthday in Isla Vista. She held my hand as we drove. It felt good.

"We'll go to Cape Cod," said Scarlet. "I love it there. My parents aren't too hot on the idea of you guys being here."

"How hot are they?" Sam asked.

"It's just that my mom thinks you're all drug addicts."

"Is she going to check us for track marks?" Sam laughed.

"If anyone's a drug addict, it's you," laughed Anna.

"What's that supposed to mean?"

"You're the one with the parents who found your weed, remember?"

"Shut up!" she blurted.

"Come on, Scarlet. We all know about it."

"It's mostly my mom. She thinks everyone from California is a drug addict. She's Catholic."

"Good thing she doesn't judge people," Anna laughed.

"I'm sorry, but she's just old."

"Who cares what your old mom thinks?" said Sam.

"I'm just warning everyone about her."

"Don't worry about it," I said, trying to cheer her up. "Your mom won't even know we're around." We all nodded.

"Call up your friends, Scarlet," said Anna. "See what's going on tonight."

"I think I know of a party across town," said Scarlet.

Scarlet drove through the darkness. She turned down a narrow dirt road to a white colonial house. I sat in the car for a moment while the others unpacked. I didn't want to go inside. I wanted to go home, but I didn't have a clue where we were.

I caught up with Cassidy just as she was walking up the gravel walkway and pushed past her. I didn't want to be the last inside.

Everyone was standing at the bottom of the stairs looking up at Scarlet's father. He was a large Irish man with a red face. Scarlet had forgotten to tell us that he was the police chief for the town.

"Dad, I had a little trouble in Boston yesterday," Scarlet admitted.

"I told you not to go there but you never listen to me," yelled the Chief.

"I left my wallet at the hotel and when I came back for it, it was gone."

"How much money did you have in it?"

"Only forty dollars," she lied. "I also lost my license."

"Well then, you're not going out tonight."

"What are you talking about? My friends are here."

"You're grounded!"

"Everyone just got here!"

"That doesn't matter."

"That's not fair!" Scarlet whined.

"Fair has nothing to do with it! Life's not fair! You're grounded!" The Chief stormed upstairs.

Scarlet turned to us, on the verge of tears. "I'm really sorry."

"I don't think I've ever been grounded before," laughed Anna.

"I'll go talk to him," Scarlet said.

"Who cares," I said. "What have you got to drink?"

"Yeah, there's plenty to eat in the kitchen. Help yourself. I've got to talk with my dad."

We went into the kitchen while Scarlet went upstairs.

"My parents would never do this to me," said Delilah in disbelief.

Sam shook his head. "This is unbelievable."

"I know what you mean," I said. "There's no liquor in these cabinets."

Delilah took some bread from the cabinet. "My parents would never embarrass me in front of my friends."

"I thought all parents did that?" said Anna.

"Not mine. Never."

"We might as well make the best of it and just start all over tomorrow."

"This sucks," said Sam.

Delilah made me a ham sandwich. I sat down at the kitchen table with the others and waited for Scarlet to come back downstairs. When she did, it was obvious that she'd been crying. I felt bad for her.

Everyone went upstairs to sleep. Delilah and I stayed up. It was nice to be with someone. I felt so alone. Scarlet had gone to bed without kissing me good night. I could feel the distance between us.

"How's it going with Scarlet?" asked Delilah.

"I'm getting a strange vibe from her."

"I'm getting the same vibe from Sam. He's acting funny."

"Maybe Sam and Scarlet are cheating on us?"

Delilah laughed. "Then we'd have to get together just to get back at them."

I liked her idea. It numbed my pain briefly. "Okay," I half-laughed.

"Just give it another day, Jack. I'm sure it'll work out."

"I don't have a choice. I'm stuck here."

Delilah kissed me and disappeared upstairs.

CHAPTER 2

I awoke to Sam rummaging around the room in a nicotine frenzy. He was packing his bags.

Sam owned three plain white shirts, two pairs of faded blue jeans, a carton of cigarettes, and a Zippo lighter. That was it.

"This place is driving me nuts," said Sam. "I've got to get out of here. Get up, Jack. Let's go." Sam picked up his bags and left the room.

"Sure thing," I mumbled.

"I'll meet you outside!" Sam yelled, halfway down the stairs. I got out of bed and paused in the doorway to rub my eyes.

Cassidy came out of the bathroom. She was naked except for a towel around her head. She let out a scream and darted into Scarlet's room. I continued down the stairs.

Delilah was in the kitchen carefully spreading cream cheese on a bagel. I sat down next to her and watched her for a moment.

"Who just screamed?" she asked.

I shrugged. "I don't know."

"Scarlet's parents probably have people locked in the attic."

"Where is Scarlet?" I asked.

"She went to get another license with her father. Do you want me to make you a bagel?"

"No thanks. I'm not hungry."

"What about some coffee?"

"I'm fine."

"Are you sure?"

"I'll get something later," I said. I got up to explore the house. I wandered down the hall towards the front door. The house was big. There was a parlor to the right with a red satin rope across the entry and a "Do not enter" sign. A Catholic shrine sat in the corner. The parlor was spotless with two red chairs, a red couch, and a grand piano in it. To the left of the parlor was the dining room with a long wooden table in the center. There were six chairs around the table and pink roses sitting in the center.

I went outside to the deck. There was a table and chairs with an umbrella. I stood on the porch for a moment and looked up into the blue sky. The sun felt good. The backyard seemed to go on forever, with trees off in the distance marking the property. There was a pond past the trees. I spotted a bench under a tree and walked across the grass to sit in the shade. I sat down next to a garden that was surrounded by giant sunflowers. There were two cats poking around the garden, trying to catch a bird that had landed a few feet away. The bird flew away just as they pounced.

Sam was sitting on the front steps smoking a cigarette and throwing pebbles in the air. There was a small wall made from stones that lined the driveway. I hopped up on it.

"What the hell are you doing?" asked Sam.

"Nothing," I said.

"We'll never get to Jersey unless Scarlet gets back here. When's she getting back?"

"Hell, if I know. Nobody ever tells me anything."

"Well, she is your girlfriend."

"I'm not sure if she is my girlfriend anymore."

"Oh, poor guy."

I went back inside to see Delilah. Just as I turned the corner, Cassidy came screaming up from the cellar. She leaped into my arms. "Get them off me!" Cassidy screamed.

"Get what off you?"

"Fleas!"

"Get them off yourself," I said, prying her away.

She jumped around and swatted them off her legs.

"They probably love the hair on your legs," said Delilah, laughing.

"It's not funny. They're all over me!"

"Don't go down there again."

"I'm never going down there, ever! I promise."

I went upstairs and took a shower. I combed my hair and put my bags in the closet so the room looked neat. I was sitting on the edge of the bed when Scarlet walked in. I looked up and noticed her wet hair.

"Were you just in the shower?" I asked.

"Yeah, I got back a little while ago. Who was screaming?"

I shrugged. "I didn't hear anything. Where's your father?"

"He went back to work."

"Did you get your license?"

"Yeah."

"So we're not grounded?" I asked.

Scarlet pouted. "I said I was sorry."

"I don't care."

"Get ready. We're leaving in five minutes."

"I am ready."

She turned to leave. I grabbed her and swung her around into my arms. Her wet hair wrapped around my fingers. I pressed my lips against hers and held her tightly. It was a long kiss.

I let go and moved my hands down her back until they were on her hips. I drew my head back and gazed into her blue eyes as if I was waiting for her to faint.

"Did you miss me?" I asked.

"Maybe." Scarlet smiled. She dragged her finger across my chest. I let go. She left me feeling complete again. All the emptiness was gone.

I walked downstairs glowing. Sam was leaning against the Jeep drawing circles in the dirty windows.

"What are you so happy about?" he asked.

"I'm just happy."

"Are you stoned? Can I have some?"

"No."

"Have you been drinking?"

"No."

"You look like you're drunk."

"You're dying to get out of here. What's the problem?"

"I just don't like this place. I mean look at it. There aren't any fences around here. It frightens me. They don't even lock their doors at night."

"I like it here," I said.

"You've been here one day." He gave me a disgusted look. "Of course you do."

The girls came out and we piled in the Jeep for a trip to Boston. I was lucky to get the window seat, although a piece of metal kept jabbing me in the side. It was difficult to enjoy anything in Scarlet's car. The Jeep was so old that it couldn't go past seventy without shaking violently. There was a smell from the back that only got worse the hotter the Jeep got. Pesticides had been spilled in the back and she'd never been able to get rid of the smell.

"I was wondering, you guys," said Cassidy. "When I was little the boys used to tease me because they said I had a big chest."

"Where the hell did that come from?" asked Sam.

"Well, it just gave me a complexion from all the teasing." The car erupted into laughter again.

"You mean a complex," Sam said.

"Where are we going?" asked Cassidy.

"We're going to the subway because I can't drive my car into Boston," said Scarlet.

"Why not?"

"My dad won't let me."

"How's he going to find out?"

"I told him we were going to church—"

We all laughed.

"He might," protested Scarlet.

"What if something happens to the car?"

"What, does he run your life or something?" asked Anna.

"No, but if he found out I took the car into Boston, he'd take it away for good. Then we'd never be able to go anywhere."

"You need to move out of the house," said Delilah, confident she had solved the problem. "You're nineteen."

"I'm going to once school starts. My mom and I aren't getting along. We're fighting all the time." Scarlet was going back to California when the summer was over. We were going to live together.

"It sounds like your whole family hates you," said Sam with a smirk.

Scarlet sighed. "It's really beginning to feel that way."

"That's just life," said Delilah.

"Yeah, I guess," said Scarlet. "We'll have fun in Boston while Sam fixes his car."

I thought about hanging around with Sam but I wanted to be with Scarlet. We parked and waited for the blue line into the city. The train station was dirty and deserted.

"Why didn't we just drive to Boston?" asked Cassidy.

"I already told you. Besides, the meter maids are ruthless."

"There's no way Boston is more dangerous than this train station," said Sam.

"Yeah, this place is shady," said Anna.

"Look at all the trash on the train tracks. All those cigarette butts."

"Those damn smokers," Sam said, lighting a cigarette.

"And look at that guy selling doughnuts over there. Is this where your dad works, Scarlet?"

"Not funny."

We all laughed.

The subway was noisy with the hustle of commuters, the newspaper stands, the candy vendors, the street musicians, and the religious freaks. Sam got off the train twenty minutes later. We were going to meet him in front of the comic bookstore on Newberry Street at five o'clock. He was going to drive us back to Scarlet's car at the train station. Sam jumped off without saying a word to Delilah. He gave me a haunting wave. The girls and I got off the train at Boston square. The buildings covered the sky, making it cold.

"I think you guys will love this place," said Scarlet.

"It's so cold," Cassidy whined.

"It'll warm up when we get to the square."

I stopped to admire the cobble stone streets.

"How old are they?" asked Cassidy.

"Pretty old," I nodded.

"Like a hundred years?"

"Colonial times."

She giggled. "What's that mean?"

I pinched her arm. "I don't know. I'm so cold."

She smiled. "You're crazy."

Scarlet took us to an outdoor food court. The girls got clam chowder. Scarlet didn't want to eat with me.

I took a walk and found a restaurant. I sat down at the bar. There were two men sitting on stools next to me, heckling the piano player. The piano player asked them to come up. The two drunks sang an Irish song. The crowd loved them. They waved for me to join them. I had a good voice. We sang "Oh, Danny Boy." The crowd loved us. It was the best time I had ever had. It felt good to be wanted.

Scarlet found me and pulled me outside. "What were you doing in there?" she asked.

"Singing."

"You're making a fool of yourself.

"We were just having fun."

"You were singing with strangers."

"I know."

"You're embarrassing yourself."

We caught up with the others. The girls stopped to listen to a homeless man ramble about the end of the world. He looked like Jesus. The girls had small cereal box samples from the food court that they gave him.

"I don't have any money," said Cassidy. "But you can have my cereal."

"Here's a dollar so you can buy some milk," said Delilah.

"God bless you," Jesus said.

"No, my good man," laughed Anna. "God bless you and enjoy that cereal."

"God bless all of you."

We left Jesus to catch the train.

The streetlights came on as the corporate people marched down the street in comfortable sneakers. The men hurried past with loose-fitting ties hanging half-beaten around their necks.

We rode the blue line to Newberry Street and looked around in the shops. The streets were crowded.

"I want a new hat," said Delilah, as we walked along the street.

Delilah bought a white boating hat with a drawstring and little metal holes. She looked cute. Anna bought a straw hat with a sunflower on it. Cassidy bought a burgundy beret.

"You want us to look good, don't you?" asked Anna.

"I don't care," I said.

"We do," said Anna. "We're trying to get some guys."

"Well then those hats will have them flocking around you any moment now."

"That's what I thought."

"Where's Scarlet?" I asked.

"She'll meet us at the bookstore."

I saw Scarlet enter the bookstore down the block. I followed her inside. I found her in the back of the store reading a book.

"Did Sam get here yet?" I asked.

"No."

"Remember when you used to read to me?"

"Yeah, I remember. You never seemed too interested in it."

It was true. I hated poetry.

"I was just pretending." I leaned in to kiss her, but she turned away.

"Sure, you were," she scoffed.

"What's going on between us?" I asked.

"What do you mean?"

"I came here to see you. I love you. You're treating me like a stranger."

She looked angry.

"Do you want me to be honest?" she asked.

"No, I want you to lie to me." I really wanted her to lie. I knew it was over. The last thing I wanted to hear was the truth.

"We're three thousand miles away from each other," she said awkwardly.

"I know. That's why I'm here, now."

"I'm not going back to Isla Vista in the fall. I'm staying here. I think we should just be friends."

My heart sank. I hated her for telling me the truth. I felt like an idiot for waiting so long to hear her tell me it was over. Nothing in my wildest dreams could have prepared me for that moment of darkness.

"I completely agree," I mumbled.

"Do you really?" Her eyes brightened.

I turned away in shame. "Whatever you want."

"Wonderful."

I could feel the fragments of my existence fading away. I tried to act like I wasn't crushed. I didn't want her to know how much I was hurting.

I wanted to take back the whole conversation. I had been so blind. I wished I never met her. I felt betrayed, rejected, and alone.

We waited hours for Sam, but he never showed. We stood around trying to think of an excuse for Sam. No one wanted to believe the worst.

"Maybe his car never got fixed," said Cassidy.

"Maybe he's stuck in traffic," said Anna.

"Maybe he got the plan wrong," said Scarlet.

"Maybe he's dead," I added.

"Not funny," Delilah snapped.

"I'm only trying to help." I was miserable. I wanted everyone to be miserable. I knew I'd hurt Delilah, but I didn't care. I knew Sam was gone. I wished I'd gone with him. Sam had seen everything that I didn't want to see. I hated him for leaving me but envied him for leaving.

"Let's go back to the car and see if he's there," said Scarlet.

"I think we should wait a little longer," said Delilah.

"We've been here for three hours," complained Anna.

"I'm sure he'll be back at the car," said Cassidy, trying to comfort Delilah.

"Let's get out of here," Scarlet said, putting her arm around me.

"What are you doing?" I asked, staring at her arm.

"We can still have a little fun, can't we?" she smiled.

I stopped walking. Scarlet skipped off. I hated her for being so devoid of emotions.

Sam wasn't at the car when we got back. Delilah cried. I held her.

"At least there's one less person in the car," Anna pointed out.

"What do we do now?" asked Delilah.

"I don't want to go back to your house," said Cassidy.

"Let's drive out to Cape Cod," suggested Scarlet.

We stopped off at three hotels, but they were all booked because of a computer convention.

"We tried the hotels," I said to Scarlet. "Now let's get some beer."

"We only have twenty minutes."

"What are you talking about? It's only 10:40 pm."

"Liquor stores close at eleven around here."

"What kind of place is this?" Anna demanded.

"Who ever heard a place not selling after eleven?" I said.

"It's the East Coast," said Scarlet. "Blue laws."

"If this is live free or die country, why are they trying to kill me?"

Anna grabbed my shoulder. "You hang in there kid and we'll get some booze into you. Don't you worry!"

"I knew I could count on you."

The clock was ticking as we passed tiny towns and stretches of farmland. It was five minutes to eleven when Anna spotted a neon sign. "It's up on the right."

Scarlet sounded relieved. "I see it."

Anna and I ran inside. I grabbed some beer and a liter of vodka. I took it up to the counter where an old man had been watching us. Anna brought over a bottle of wine and set it on the counter.

"You got any identification?" the old man asked.

"I sure do." I fished my license out of my wallet and handed it to him.

He handed it back. "No out of state licenses."

"What are you talking about?"

"I don't have the book so I can't look it up."

"You don't need the book because it's real."

"It doesn't matter. I need the book."

"Take my money and keep the change. Just close the door behind us. That way we're both happy."

"I just can't do that, son."

"I'm not your fucking son."

"Take it easy, Jack," said Anna.

"No, I've had a real fucked up day and now all I want is to buy some liquor! The only thing stopping me from being happy is this old bastard!"

"You're going to have to leave," he growled.

"You fucking leave, old man!"

He pulled out a pistol and pointed it at me. Anna pulled me towards the door.

"Come on, Jack. Let's just go."

"This state is fucked in the head!"

The old man locked the door behind us. My spirit had been broken.

We headed back to the highway and found a hotel. There was a frail man complaining about the room price at the counter. It was the last room. He left it to us. The manager was a large woman with a frown on her face.

"I'd like a room," I asked politely.

"You need a credit card to rent a room here," she growled.

"You're in luck," I said. "I just happen to have one right here in my wallet."

"That's nice but you need to be twenty-one to rent a room in our establishment."

"This must be your lucky day. I'm twenty-one. I was cursed with a young face."

"Very well then, I'll write up the paperwork."

"Is there a wedding upstairs?" I inquired. "I hear music."

"That's the bar on the second floor."

"I thought bars closed at 11:00 around here?"

"Just liquor stores. Bars are open until 12:30."

I contained my excitement and shot Anna a look.

I grabbed my license off the counter. I gave Anna my bag.

"Where are you going?" she asked.

"Upstairs to get drunk."

"You're my hero."

I dashed up the spiral staircase and burst through double oak doors into the bar. I made my way over to the circular bar as a disco ball flickered a multitude of colors over the carpeted walls. I sat down on a stool. A deejay spun records in a polyester suit. There had been a wedding reception. The newlyweds were the only ones left. They slow danced to a country song.

"What'll it be?" the bartender asked.

"Two beers."

"I need some ID."

I showed it to him.

"Sorry, I can't take ones from out of state."

"Are you serious?"

"I'll lose my job."

"I'll lose my sanity." I leaned over the bar so he could hear me better. "You look like a reasonable guy. I just traveled three thousand miles to have my girlfriend break up with me. I've got problems. Please, give me a drink."

"I hear you," he said, nodding his head.

"Thank you."

I didn't believe in guardian angels but the bartender was the closest I had ever come.

Delilah walked in and sat down next to me. "Hey handsome," she whispered.

"Damn, am I glad to see you."

"You are?"

"Sure. Now I have someone to drink with."

Delilah kissed me on the check. I passed her one of my beers. The bartender didn't care. I was tipping him well. We drank as much as we wanted.

"How's it going with Scarlet?" she asked.

"She just wants to be friends."

"Do you want to talk about it?"

"No. It's over. I just want to get drunk."

"At least she told you. Sam just ran away."

"I'd rather have her run away."

"Do you want to dance?"

"Why not?"

We danced to a slow song. Delilah cried. I held her. It felt good. She was in as much pain as I was. I wished Delilah was mine, but she was in love with Sam.

"Last call," shouted the bartender.

We downed our drinks and stumbled back to the room holding hands. We were happy drunks. We knocked on the door of our room. Delilah pressed her head against the door like a detective.

"What do you think they're doing?" I asked. Delilah knocked again. "Open up. It's us." She knocked a few more times.

"Open the damn door," I yelled.

Cassidy slowly opened the door and stuck her head out to see if anyone was coming down the hall. "Did anyone follow you?" she inquired.

"Of course not," I said. I pushed the door open past her.

"Be quiet. Scarlet's on the phone with her parents."

Scarlet had one hand over the receiver and her index finger pressed against her lips. I went to the icebox and found a beer. I sat on the bed next to Delilah.

"Do you think she wants us to be quiet?" I whispered.

Delilah giggled. "I think so."

Scarlet shook her fist at me. I shook mine back. Delilah giggled more.

Scarlet slammed the phone down. "What was that for?" Scarlet demanded.

"Keep it down," I laughed. "You'll wake the neighbors."

"Do you want to get us all in trouble?"

"What's the big deal?" I asked.

"I was telling my dad that we were at a friend's house, not here. He'd flip out if he found out I was staying here."

"You stayed in Boston two days ago?"

"That was different."

"How so?"

"It just was. I don't like having to lie to him."

"You lie to everyone."

"Let's just drop it."

"Fine with me."

"I'm going to bed."

I got up and headed for another beer.

"Oh, no," said Scarlet. "You're not drinking my beer."

"Where did you get beer?" I demanded.

"I found it in the Jeep," she admitted.

"So, you were hiding it from us?"

"It's mine."

"You're going to sleep and we're still awake. If it makes you feel any better, I'll pay for it."

"Forget it."

"No, I'll pay for it. God forbid you be nice for once in your life."

"Just give him the beer," snapped Anna.

Anna always had my back. She understood my alcoholism. I took the beer and turned the water on in the bathroom hot tub. It was huge. Delilah followed me and took off her clothes. She was wearing a purple bra and panties. She looked amazing. I got in the tub and Delilah leaned against me. She felt good. To feel the touch of another human being was healing.

"I just have to say," said Delilah. "Even though things have gone bad, I really did miss you."

"I missed you too."

"Don't leave, Jack. Stick it out with me."

CHAPTER 3

Everyone got up early the next morning. We stopped for breakfast at a diner near Cape Cod.

"Why aren't you eating, Jack?" asked Cassidy.

"I'm not hungry."

"Have a bite of my pancakes."

Scarlet gave me a sympathetic look. "Jack, you need to eat."

I stuck a piece of toast in my mouth and smiled.

I was lovesick. To have something so close and yet so far out of reach was horrible. I sat at the table and gazed at Scarlet. Once in a while she would glance over. I would look away, but it was obvious what I was doing.

"We can stop by this boutique on the way," said Scarlet. "It's in this little town. You guys will love it. It's so cool."

The boutique was in an old Victorian house across the street from a general store. The girls went inside. I went into the general store. They didn't sell alcohol, so I bought a bag of penny candy. The clerk watched me closely with his small-town eyes.

I left the general store and sat on the porch of the boutique waiting for the girls. An old woman came out of the boutique fanning herself with a magazine.

"It's hot," she said.

"It is," I agreed.

"And you look sad."

"I am."

"Why is a young man like you so sad?"

"I don't know."

"Does it have to do with matters of the heart?"

"I guess?"

"Oh dear, it looks as if I've hit a nerve. You know what always cheers me up?"

"I haven't a clue."

"A rose. I think you need a rose." She handed me a red rose and left.

Scarlet came outside. "What were you doing talking to the owner?"

"I didn't know she was the owner. She gave me a rose."

"Why would she do that?"

"I don't know, but you can have it." I handed the rose to Scarlet, but she pushed it away.

"I don't want that," she scoffed.

I dropped the rose on the porch. Delilah walked out just as I smashed the rose with my shoe.

"I'll take the rose," said Delilah.

"Nobody gets it now," I said.

The sun was dodging in and out of the clouds as we made our way to the cape. We parked in front of a small church with a large stained-glass window that overlooked the harbor.

"What are all these people dressed up for?" Cassidy asked.

"Yeah, what's the deal?" asked Anna.

"It's *Sunday*," said Scarlet, as if we were all crazy.

"It doesn't feel like Sunday," I said.

"Like you've ever gone to church," said Scarlet.

"I went once, I think."

"I went too," insisted Anna, "but they kicked me out."

"I feel so guilty for not being in church right now," said Scarlet.

"Why?" asked Cassidy.

"I've been going to church and mass all my life."

"Religion's never been my cup of tea," said Delilah.

Anna agreed. "Me neither."

"I've lost all faith," I added.

Scarlet pointed at the church. "See that church? That's where I want to get married."

"Let's do it," I said. I was serious. I would have married her right there, but she hated me.

She looked embarrassed. "I can't marry you."

I gave her a disgusted look. "Well, I don't want to marry you either." She brushed it off like I was nothing.

"I just love that stained glass window," said Scarlet. "It's so beautiful. I want a picture of me over by that bench."

"I'll take it," said Cassidy. "Get in the picture with her, Jack."

"I don't want to be in the picture."

"Be a sport."

"I don't feel like being a sport."

"Just sit on the bench with Scarlet. Do it for me, please."

"Alright, I'll do it for you, but I'm not going to like it."

Scarlet smiled. I didn't. Cassidy snapped the photo.

"You looked away, Jack," said Cassidy.

"I didn't say I was going to smile."

"Then let me take another picture."

"Forget it. I only agreed to one picture, and you already took it." I was being a child and it felt good.

Scarlet got up from the bench. "Let's just go to the beach."

"Where is the beach?" asked Cassidy.

Scarlet pointed. "It's over that way. Like a mile."

"Why can't we drive there?"

"We'd never find a parking spot."

The girls went inside a store. I ducked inside a bar for a drink. Drinking was all I had left. There were two guys in tuxedos at the end of the bar. One was passed out. The other turned to me.

"Could you help me out here, buddy?" he asked.

"What do you need?"

"Just grab his legs. We've got to get him out of here. He's supposed to be getting married in five minutes."

The groom opened his eyes and grabbed me. "I don't want to get married!" he screamed.

"Okay," I said.

He latched onto my leg. "Don't let them take me, please!"

I slapped him. "Shut up. You're getting married whether you like it or not."

"Just let me sleep some more on the bar."

"Easy there," said the best man. "I just need your help carrying him, not beating him."

"Right. Sorry."

A limo pulled up and we tossed him in the back. I waved goodbye. I was jealous he was getting married. I wanted to marry Scarlet. I wanted to be loved.

"What was all that about?" asked Delilah, hugging me from behind.

"I have no idea."

She held up a Cape Cod sweatshirt. "Look what I bought."

"A souvenir to remind you of this hell-hole. I like it." We walked along the boardwalk until we came to stairs that led down to the beach. There wasn't sand on the beach, but broken shells. It was difficult to walk on. The shells were in chunks and kept stabbing my feet.

"What's on the ground?" Cassidy asked.

"They're shells," said Scarlet.

"Where's the sand?"

"In the ocean."

"I want sand. Nice fine little grains of sand."

"It won't be bad when you lay your towel down."

"I don't have a towel."

"Why not?"

"I didn't think New Hampshire had an ocean," said Cassidy.

"I told you we were going to other places besides my house."

"You never mentioned the beach."

"Don't worry," I interrupted. "I brought towels for everyone."

I handed her a towel from my backpack.

"Where'd you get all those towels?" demanded Scarlet.

"From the hotel."

"You stole them?"

"Of course not, I borrowed them. I just don't intend to return them." I ran into the ocean. I fell in over my head a few feet in. The water was freezing. The East Coast beaches were different from the West Coast beaches but people didn't mind. They adjusted. I hurried back to the warmth of my towel. Delilah laid down next to me.

"Here's some candy," she said.

"Thanks."

"I got you a fake tattoo. Put it on."

"Only if you put yours on first."

She licked the paper and slapped it on my neck. She laughed. "I love it."

Anna looked up from her book. "There are no cute guys on this beach. Only Jack, and he doesn't really count."

"Thanks," I said.

It was cold and gray when Scarlet kicked my ribs. I sat up for a moment in a daze. The girls shook the sand from their towels and walked towards the Jeep. I had been asleep for an hour.

"We're leaving," Scarlet scoffed.

"Good."

"Come on, Jack!" yelled Delilah, in the distance.

"At least someone cares," I mumbled.

I caught up with Delilah. We walked behind the others gazing across the bay towards Martha's Vineyard. The wind had picked up and had blown the clouds away, exposing the sun.

"Why are we leaving so early?" Cassidy asked.

"We're going to foul mouth," yelled Anna.

I laughed. "Don't you mean Faulmouth?"

"No, I mean foul mouth. In foul mouth, we're going to the aquarium. We've got to leave now if we want to get there before it closes."

I fell asleep in the Jeep as we twisted through tree-shaded back roads.

The aquarium was closed for renovation. A wooden cut-out of a pirate with knee-high stockings happily tossing anchovies into the air spelled out CLOSED.

"I thought you said you'd been here before," said Cassidy to Scarlet.

"It's not my fault they're fixing the place," said Scarlet.

"I wanted to see the seals," Cassidy pouted.

Scarlet took us to a lobster place where old sea captains went to dunk their dentures in stale black coffee. There were lobster traps and fishnets glued to the walls. I gazed at the old Formica floors. The girls got lobster rolls.

"What's wrong with you?" demanded Scarlet.

"Where would you like me to begin?" I said.

"Why aren't you eating?"

"I'm not hungry."

"You need to eat."

"I know."

"I'm going to get you a lobster roll."

I enjoyed the attention, but I didn't want a lobster roll. I hated seafood.

I slept the rest of the way back. Scarlet stopped me in the upstairs hallway of her home.

"Where are you going?" she asked.

"To sleep," I said.

"After you meet my mom."

"I'd rather eat sandpaper. I thought your mom hated us?"

"She wants to meet all of you."

"What for? What am I going to tell her? That I like playing badminton and bathing my ankles in yogurt?"

"Just come down to the living room and say hello."

"What's going on?" asked Delilah, coming up the stairs.

"Scarlet's parents want to meet us."

"I guess we better go down there."

"Yeah, this ought to be fun," I mumbled.

"I wish we had a place to hide," Delilah added.

Scarlet's parents were sitting in the dark watching reruns of *Archie Bunker's Place*. They directed their questions at me like I was a cult leader.

"How was your day?" they asked.

"Fine," I said.

"How was Cape Cod?"

"Fine."

"How do you like New England?"

"Fine."

"Why are you so quiet?"

"Just tired."

"They say you've got to watch out for the quiet ones."

I forced a smile.

The phone rang and Scarlet went to answer it. I'd never been so happy to hear the phone ring in my entire life. It was like a bell ending the first round of a boxing match. We bolted upstairs. Delilah was right behind me when I got into my room.

"That was bizarre," she said, trying to catch her breath.

Scarlet came running up the stairs. "I found a party," she said.

Anna laughed, "Hey, there's a party in Scarlet's mouth and everyone's coming."

"Shut up," Scarlet snapped.

"Are there going to be any guys there?" asked Anna.

"Of course."

"Cute ones?"

"You'll just have to wait and see."

I went to my room. Delilah came in and modeled a dress for me. She was stunning.

"So, what do you think?" she asked.

"You look good."

"I don't want to look good. I want to look hot."

"You look hot."

"Are you serious?"

"Would I lie to you?"

"No, I think you're the most honest guy I know."

Scarlet didn't bother to ask me how she looked but I thought she looked incredible. She had her hair pulled back in a braid.

We drove off to the party.

"You forgot Cassidy," laughed Anna.

Scarlet stopped the Jeep. "Where is she?"

"She's still getting ready."

"Why does it take her so long?"

"Who knows?"

Cassidy ran down the street and got into the Jeep.

"I have something to tell all of you before we get there," said Scarlet.

"Is your father coming with us?" Anna asked.

"It's about my friends, or I mean, people on the East Coast."

"They're space aliens collecting human cargo because their planet is hungry."

"No, but they are different."

"If they're like you I think we can handle it," Anna assured her.

"I'm not like my friends. These friends are very different."

"Why should it bother us?"

"I just want to warn you."

"You've been warning us since we got here."

"I just want you all to have fun."

"I'm having the time of my life," I added.

"Be quiet!" Scarlet snapped. "I'm trying to explain that they're a bit weird."

We stopped to get beer at Shaw's market. I went inside carrying a list from the girls. I grabbed a shopping cart and filled it with liquor.

"I'm going to have to see your ID," said the cashier, when I got to the counter.

She fondled it like she was caressing the expired wrapper of a lubricated condom. "What's this?" she asked.

"It's a driver's license."

"Is it from the United States?"

"It says California across the top."

"Oh." She turned to the old lady behind me. "Have you ever seen anything like this in your life?"

"For heaven sakes, never!" gasped the old broad.

"I'm going to have to call the manager on this one." Customers gathered around. My license was the talk of the town.

"It checks out," said the cashier, handing it back.

A man behind me reached out his hand. "Can I see that thing?"

I pushed him back. "Some other time," I explained. "I'm in a hurry."

Scarlet pulled up to a home that looked like hers.

"This looks just like your house Scarlet," said Cassidy.

"No, it doesn't," Scarlett scoffed.

"It's the same color."

I nodded to Cassidy. "Her father owns this home too."

"Really?"

Scarlet let out a puff of frustration. "Let's just go in," she said. "They probably won't have any beer."

We jumped out of the Jeep.

"It's the big moment," I whispered to Cassidy.

"What do you mean?" she asked.

"When East meets the West. The big showdown. The matchup of old friends and new friends."

"Is it that serious?" Cassidy asked.

"It seems that way, but don't you worry. I'm going to get really drunk and make a complete fool out of myself."

"For reals?"

We followed Scarlet around the side of the house and in through the back door. There were two guys and two girls sitting in a circle drinking wine. They were dressed like Mennonites. The room was silent until a cute blonde girl named Holly recognized Scarlet.

"Hey, Scarlet. I'm glad you came," said Holly.

"Thanks."

"It's great to see you. We have a lot of beer. Help yourself."

I gave Scarlet a look. "Did you hear that, Scarlet? They have beer. She's nice and wants us to drink her beer. Isn't that incredible?"

Scarlet sighed. "I heard."

Delilah shuffled a deck of cards and suggested that we play a drinking game.

Delilah dealt the cards. I had played many card games with Delilah. She was a great card cheat. She gave me the good cards. We won every game. I loved her for that.

Scarlet knew we were cheating but was powerless to do anything about it. I watched the blood drain from her face. She hated that we were taking her East Coast friends for suckers.

By eleven o'clock, Scarlet wanted to leave: "Everyone goes home early here."

"What, are they religious?" asked Anna.

"No," Scarlet said in disgust.

I jumped up and grabbed Anna. We were both drunk. We danced around the room. She jumped on my back. Scarlet pleaded with us to stop.

We galloped outside, then around the front lawn until I tripped and hit the ground.

"Are you alright?" I asked Anna.

"Yeah, that was fun," she laughed. "Look a dog!" Anna got up and hugged a golden retriever.

Scarlet followed us outside. "What are you two doing?" Scarlet demanded.

Anna turned around. "I'm hugging a dog, you idiot. Can't you see that?"

"What for?"

"Because I love animals more than people."

"Just get in the Jeep."

"Can I keep the dog?"

"No!"

I had a deep connection with Anna. She knew my pain. She was my partner against Scarlet. I owed her my life.

Scarlet took us to the Elvis Café. The place was shaped like Elvis' face, and the front door was his mouth. Scarlet introduced us to a waiter dressed liked Elvis. I had a feeling that the Elvis waiter was Scarlet's new boyfriend. She looked at him the way she used to look at me. Scarlet left us at a table to talk to him in the kitchen.

I stumbled outside and threw up in the bushes. Cassidy followed me and jumped on the hood of a car parked nearby. A guy got out and yelled at her.

"What are you doing?" he demanded.

Cassidy turned to me and laughed. "Jack, go kick his ass."

The guy pulled out a knife and motioned to me. "You got a problem?" he demanded.

I moved towards him and put the knife to my stomach. "Do it," I said. "I don't care anymore."

He pulled the knife away. "You're crazy!"

He got in his car and drove off.

Cassidy yelled after him, "Loser!"

Scarlet ran out. "What is wrong with you, Jack?" she demanded.

"You broke my heart!" I yelled.

Scarlet didn't say a word on the way home. She went straight to bed. Delilah and I stayed up. She made me a sandwich. We shared a bottle of vodka I took from the party. I held her while she cried over Sam.

CHAPTER 4

The girls were having lunch at the kitchen table when I woke up.

"What time is it?" I asked.

"One thirty," said Delilah.

"I've got to start getting up earlier."

"Maybe if you didn't sleep so late," said Scarlet.

Anna cut in. "Don't worry, Jack. We all just got up."

"No, we didn't," insisted Scarlet.

"So, what happened last night?" I asked.

Scarlet turned towards the window like a victim. "I don't want to talk about it."

"Good," said Anna. "You can just listen."

"You got drunk," said Cassidy with bright eyes.

"Let's just forget about it," said Scarlet.

"Let's not," I said.

"Did we embarrass you last night?" laughed Delilah.

"Let's get ready to go," said Scarlet.

Scarlet drove us to Maine to swim in a river. Everything was bright red and green.

"They call it the color," explained Scarlet. "People come here just to drive around and look at the trees."

Cassidy interrupted. "Did you ever get your hair caught in your armpits as a kid when you wore pajamas?"

"No, I didn't," said Scarlet, parking the Jeep.

"Why'd we stop?" asked Cassidy.

"'Cause I'm not driving down the train tracks. It's a big fine to have your car on the train tracks. It's kind of dangerous if a train comes too."

"Just move your car when you hear the train coming," said Cassidy.

"No. We're walking."

We walked the tracks towards the trestle. Delilah and I walked along the tracks holding a stick in between us for balance. We did rather well until Anna jabbed me in the side with another stick. I fell off the tracks.

We reached the trestle and looked down at the water. It was thirty feet to the river below. I was afraid of heights and Scarlet knew it. She had taken us there to spite me. She wanted me to die.

Scarlet and Anna jumped over together.

"Are you going in?" asked Delilah.

"Looks kind of far down," I said.

"All you've got to do is jump. It'll be over in a second."

"Thanks."

Delilah turned and leaped over the side. I closed my eyes and jumped over. In seconds I was submerged in the murky green water. Delilah grabbed me. She kissed me before we broke the surface. It was nice. We swam to the riverbank. I pulled her up and helped her over the jagged rocks covered with moss.

I held her for a moment. Mosquitoes killed the mood. They followed us up the trail to the trestle. A train buzzed by.

"Watch out for the mosquitoes," warned Scarlet.

"Why?" asked Cassidy.

"They'll eat you alive."

"They can't be as bad as the bugs in your basement."

"The bugs are really bad this time of year. Especially along the trees."

Scarlet's other friends arrived. One of them was the Elvis waiter. She looked at him again the way she used to look at me. She had a gift for being fake. She smiled and laughed. She touched his arm the way she used to touch mine. Elvis climbed to the top of the trestle and dove into the river. Scarlet didn't take her eyes off him.

We walked back to the Jeep.

Anna spotted a pair of old white underwear beside the tracks. She picked them up with a stick and chased Scarlet to the Jeep. Cassidy ran after them. Delilah and I laughed. We held hands and walked the tracks in silence. It was nice to be alone with Delilah. We stopped off at Long John Silver's. I didn't bother to put on a shirt. We went inside. The manager kicked me out. Scarlet followed me outside.

"I don't see why you can't follow the rules," Scarlet said.

"How am I supposed to know the rules? I'm not from here."

"It's different here."

"No shit."

"I'll order you something."

"I'm not hungry."

"You're never hungry," mumbled Scarlet.

"I wonder why?"

I waited by the Jeep. Scarlet acted like nothing had happened when she came back. On the way home, we passed Jesus standing on a street corner with a sign around his neck that read JOHN 3:16. He looked like the same Jesus from Boston.

"What's his sign mean?" asked Cassidy.

"I think it means as long as you believe, you'll go to heaven," said Scarlet.

"You're the one who goes to church all the time," said Cassidy.

"I don't know. Look it up in a Bible."

"You can have one of the Bibles I took from the hotel," I said.

"I hope I didn't just hear what I thought I heard," said Scarlet, looking at me in the rear-view mirror.

"Like they don't have rooms full of Bibles? Hotels are required to carry them. I'm sure they can spare a few. They want you to take them."

"Is that true?" asked Cassidy.

"Would I lie to you?"

"No."

"Well, it sure doesn't help when you steal the Bible from our hotel room," said Scarlet.

"I didn't steal it, I borrowed it. I just don't intend to return it. There is a difference, you know."

Delilah and I took a long walk when we got home. Scarlet's dog, Timber, followed us. He was a dopey looking yellow lab.

We didn't talk but I could feel her empathy for me. She cared about me, and I cared for her.

We strolled through the tall grass and sat by the pond as the sun went down. Birds flew by and the smell of lilac lingered in the air. God had given us a moment of peace. I was thankful for it. It was the perfect day, but we both loved someone else.

Scarlet's mom had fixed us dinner when we got back to the house. The woman hated us, but took the time to cook.

"Just come and humor her," pleaded Scarlet.

"But we already ate—remember, I embarrassed you?"

"I know but she made this big dinner for everyone."

"Isn't your brother coming home today?" I asked.

"He just pulled up with my dad."

"So, the dinner is for him?"

"Please just come downstairs and eat something. At least meet my brother."

"I already met your brother. I don't like him. He doesn't drink. I don't trust people who don't drink." Her brother had just gotten out of rehab for the third time.

Anna pointed at Scarlet and whispered to me as she made her way downstairs. "You owe me big time for this."

The girls ate fast and left me alone with Scarlet's family. I sat silently listening to her brother talk about his time in rehab. I wanted her family to like me even though I would never see them again. I excused myself and found Delilah writing postcards to her family.

"Sorry about leaving you downstairs but I couldn't deal," said Delilah. "I came up here and then got caught up writing postcards."

"It's cool."

"Do you want a postcard?"

"I don't have anyone to write to."

"You can write to me."

CHAPTER 5

The Chief picked us up at noon to take us to Kittery, Maine. Scarlet had to work. She was going to meet us later.

"You don't look like you're looking forward to today," the Chief said as I came down the stairs.

"Not really, sir. What can I say, shopping just isn't my thing."

"I know exactly what you mean. Just wait until you're married."

"I don't like to think ahead that far."

"If you make it through today, you can spend the day with me tomorrow."

"I'd like that a lot." I lied. I didn't want to hang out with him. I was hungover and my head hurt.

Cassidy sat next to me in the police cruiser. "Have you shot anyone?" Cassidy asked the Chief.

"I've had a few altercations where I've needed to use the proper force."

"Is there a big problem with the mob in Maine?"

"No, but they've got a problem with them in Boston and New York."

"Have you ever met the president?"

"Of the United States?"

"Yeah, or any movie stars?"

"Sure, I've met three presidents."

"Wow, how old are you?"

"I'll plead the fifth on that one." The Chief was patient with Cassidy. I liked him for that.

Kittery stretched on forever and sold just about everything. I knew of Kittery because Humphrey Bogart had been injured in the Navy while transferring an inmate in Kittery. I bought two boxes of golf balls for the Chief, whose birthday was that day. Cassidy had taped a sad looking birthday card to the refrigerator. I didn't want it to be the only present the Chief got for his birthday. I walked across the highway and bought some beer. I sat down by a riverbank watching the dark clouds stir in the distance. A storm was moving in. I could see the lightening. I finished the beer and met up with the girls at Coat World. Anna bought a burgundy snow jacket. It started to rain. I dozed off for a while on a bench waiting for the girls outside Shoe World. An awning kept me dry as lightening crackled in the distance.

Anna poked me. "Come on," she said. "It's time to go. You can make it buddy."

I shook my head. "No, I can't." I had sunk into a deep depression.

Scarlet arrived at six and we went to Camping World so Delilah could buy some hiking boots. I sat outside smoking a cigarette. Scarlet sat down next to me.

"What's going on?" she asked.

"Not much. How was work?"

"It was a nightmare."

"Do you want a cigarette?"

"No thanks. I can't stand those non-filters you smoke."

"Suit yourself."

"Can I ask you a question?"

I lit another cigarette. "I don't care."

"Why are you being so mean to me?"

"I didn't know I was."

"Everywhere we go you have some comment to make to me."

I felt proud that she noticed. "It makes me feel better," I said coldly.

"Well it makes me feel stupid."

"You broke up with me."

"I'm just trying to talk with you. You never listen to me."

"Maybe I don't want to."

"Christ, you're impossible."

"And you're not?"

She stormed off.

"What's wrong with Scarlet?" asked Delilah, standing behind me.

"Who knows?"

"She was trying to talk to you."

"It's a little too late for that."

"She wants to be friends."

"She's got a funny way of showing it."

"Why do you think we came to this store?"

"I thought you wanted to buy some boots?"

"We came here because Scarlet thought you'd like it."

"I hate camping."

"She was thinking of you and trying to get you to have some fun."

"I've had enough fun."

"Just promise me you won't hurt her anymore?"

"I haven't even done anything. She hurt me."

"You're being stubborn."

"I thought I was being impossible."

We drove home in silence. Scarlet heard about a party. We got back into the Jeep after dinner. Her mother made us pasta.

"I have to warn you about my friends," said Scarlet.

"Not this again," I said. Delilah put a finger over my lips.

"We've met your friends," insisted Anna.

"Yeah, but these are different friends," said Scarlet.

"Will you shut up," I said. "No one cares."

"Yeah, Scarlet," said Anna. "We don't need to hear it. They don't bother us, so shut up about it."

"They don't bother us," said Cassidy. "Just shut up."

It was nice to have everyone hate Scarlet.

The party was at a one-bedroom apartment behind a church in the middle of town. I walked into the kitchen and chugged a bottle of vodka.

"Don't drink so much," Scarlet growled.

I took a long pull off the bottle.

"He's doing this on purpose," Scarlet announced to no one. "He's trying to embarrass me."

"Leave him alone," said Anna.

"When he drinks like this he blacks out," added Scarlet. "He knows."

I lifted the bottle. It slipped through my fingers and crashed to the floor. Scarlet grabbed my arm and slapped my face. My body was so numb. I enjoyed it. I smiled. "Did that make you happy?"

"The party is over!" Scarlet yelled. "It's time for us to leave."

"It's so early!" I shouted back.

"Don't patronize me! It's time for us to leave."

It was quiet on the way home. I was getting used to the silence. Scarlet left me on the front lawn. Delilah laid down next to me.

"You're going to have to do better, Jack," said Delilah. She put her arms around me.

"I know."

CHAPTER 6

The Chief came to get us in the morning, but everyone was still asleep. He was taking us to Portsmouth to meet Scarlet.

I met him in the hallway downstairs. "Rough night?" he asked. The others were all up now, running around getting ready.

"Did Scarlet say something to you?" I asked.

"No, why?" He didn't know I slept most of the night outside.

"Oh, just wondering. It was kind of boring to tell you the truth."

"Well, we'll have fun today after we drop the girls off at Scarlet's work. Still up for it?"

"You mean spending the day with you?"

"Yeah, you don't want to hang out with a bunch of girls."

"You're right, I don't," I lied. I was horrified to be with him. I wanted to be with Scarlet.

Scarlet worked as a waitress at a restaurant down along the Piscataqua River. The restaurant was a shack on stilts that was falling apart. It had pictures of old movie stars that I'd never heard of. Most of the pictures were warped and barely visible. The outside deck was slanted to one side and creaked when walked on. I rolled a quarter under the table and watched it roll off the edge. Everyone knew the Chief.

No one knew me. Scarlet had failed to tell anyone about me.

I left with the Chief. He wanted to show me around town. "Do you surf?" asked the Chief.

"Do I surf?"

"Yeah, you know? Like in the ocean with all those other people out there in California?"

"No. I don't surf."

"I thought all you people from California surfed."

"You just met one that doesn't."

"You're not very tan either."

"I guess not."

"I thought all you California people were tan."

"The sun hasn't been coming out much lately."

"How do you like it out here?"

"I like it a lot. I'd like to live here."

"You don't want to live here because of a woman, do you?"

"No."

"Remember, they're the root of all evil."

We drove around for a while and then went to an old military base next to a golf course. It was the hide out for the cops. The golfers on the driving range aimed their shots at us.

"These bums always try to hit my car, but they haven't gotten me yet," the Chief said. "I sit off to the side and then I've got this stretch of road that I race down. That's when they try to hit the car. Idiots, I tell you. Most of them I went to high school with. All they do is play golf." He revved the engine and raced down the road. The golf balls flew past us. "There was a UFO abduction in this town. A real famous story. The Betty and Barney Hill story. Have you heard of it?"

"No."

"Look it up. Really weird."

The Chief dropped me off in Portsmouth to meet the girls. He was a good man. He could have been a monster, but he wasn't. I had forgotten where I was supposed to meet the girls. I wandered around in a panic.

Delilah grabbed me by the arm and swung me around.

"Jesus, it's good to see you," I said.

"What's wrong?" she asked. "You look nervous."

"I couldn't remember where to meet you guys. I couldn't really think."

"Don't be stupid. You found me."

"Where's Scarlet?"

"She's in a candle store."

I went inside the candle shop. Scarlet was looking at a blue candle shaped like the earth. She turned to me and said, "I like this candle, but I don't want to spend the money on it." She set the candle down and walked out.

I bought the candle and followed her outside. I handed her the candle in front of the store.

"Why did you buy this for me?" she demanded.

"I thought you wanted it."

"Not from you." She handed the candle back and walked away.

I threw the candle on the ground. It broke in two.

Scarlet's mom had dinner waiting for us when we got home. She had set a place for me in the dining room while the girls ate at the kitchen table. She didn't know Scarlet had dumped me.

Scarlet played the guitar for her parents after dinner. She had a good voice. We didn't get out of the house until ten because we watched a surf movie that Scarlet's brother was making. Scarlet's mom didn't want her to feel left out so she made us watch Scarlet in an equestrian competition from ten years ago. Watching Scarlet being thrown from a horse was entertaining.

Scarlet's friend, Holly, met us in the parking lot of Shaw's Market. Holly hit a curb, and blew out a tire. I went inside the market to get the beer.

When I got outside the girls were gone. I was left alone with Holly. She was cute but had an angry face.

I opened a beer.

"You better put that in the car and cover it," said Holly.

"Why?"

"The cops are nazis around here."

"Where did Scarlet go?" I asked.

"She went to pick someone up."

"Is she coming back?" I asked, half-scared.

"Yeah, she'll be back in a few minutes."

"Did you fix your tire?"

"No, I don't have one," said Holly.

"Your car looks rather new," I said. "Are you sure you don't have one?"

She looked at me like I was an idiot. "I looked in the back but didn't see one."

"Do you have a tire iron?"

"What's that?"

"Let me look in the trunk."

"There isn't a spare tire," said Holly, rolling her eyes.

"I'm sure you have something back there."

I opened the trunk. I ran my fingers along the edges. The spare tire and a tire iron were under the carpet. "We've got a problem." I said.

"What did you do now?" she scoffed, shaking her head.

"I found the spare tire and jack."

"Oh, my God! You did not! Just totally saved me. I love you!" She threw her arms around me. I changed the tire.

Scarlet came back. Holly seemed to change into a lovely person. She wanted me to ride with her. She opened a beer and handed it to me.

"What about the cops?" I asked.

"Fuck 'em." she said.

We drove up a narrow dirt road that led to a house on stilts. There were giant pine trees around it. Holly took me by the hand and led me inside. She sat me down at the kitchen table and opened another beer for me. She talked to me the way Scarlet used to. We talked all night. She put her hand on my leg. The party got bigger and louder. Holly kissed me. Scarlet ran over. I never looked up. I was too happy to care. Holly had filled the void.

"I see you've met my friend," said Scarlet. "I brought him here."

"Oh, did he come with you?" Holly asked. "He's really cute."

"He didn't tell you?"

"No, he didn't even tell me his name."

"This is Jack. He's my old boyfriend." It was the first time Scarlet had acknowledged knowing me.

"Like I said, really cute," said Holly.

There was a heavy tension between them.

"She doesn't like me anymore," I added.

"Do you still love him?" asked Holly.

It was the perfect blow to her ego. Scarlet didn't answer. I thought for a moment that she might not have heard Holly, but then I saw her biting her lower lip. She couldn't answer.

"Well, it's time to go." Scarlet said in a low, angry tone.

"I want to stay here," I said.

"Fine. I don't care. Good luck finding your way home. I'm not coming back to pick you up."

She had called my bluff.

"Why don't you stay the night?" Holly asked.

"My dad will be pissed that you didn't come home with us." Scarlet said.

"I guess you're right." I hung my head like a batter who had just struck out.

I kissed Holly goodbye and ran out to the Jeep. I sat next to Delilah.

"Who was that girl you were with?" she asked.

"Oh, just someone I'm in love with." I said, feeling confident.

"What about Scarlet?"

"Who's that?"

Delilah laughed. "I told you everything would be better."

Scarlet was stoned and drove home slowly. The Chief was waiting up for us. Delilah had passed out, and I carried her past him into the house.

"Do you know how late it is, young lady?" the Chief barked.

"It's not that late, dad," whined Scarlet.

"You were supposed to be home at twelve."

"Why?"

"You have a curfew. There are a lot of crazy people out at this time of night."

"Oh Dad, everything is fine."

"No, it's not. It's not fine when I must wait up for you. We're going to have a talk about this right now!"

"Can't we talk about it tomorrow?" Scarlet begged.

"No, right now!"

We left Scarlet and went upstairs. Delilah was drunk and sad. She laid down on my bed. I held her again while she cried about Sam. I could hear the Chief yelling at Scarlet. It was nice to hear Scarlet get yelled at. She deserved it. The Chief was concerned but he wasn't consistent. He got enraged every few days. He liked us but he didn't know the depths of our alcoholism.

CHAPTER 7

Anna was eating a bowl of Fruity Pebbles cereal in the kitchen when I got up.

"School starts next week," she said.

"What?"

"I said, I think it's strange that school starts next week."

"That's the best news I've ever heard."

"What's with you?"

"Don't you see," I said, excited. "There is an end to this. There is something for me to look forward to."

"You've never looked forward to school in your life."

"It just never crossed my mind. I'm not stuck here. I've got something to go back to. I'm so happy I could kiss you right now."

"Well, please don't," she said, shielding her face with the bowl of cereal.

The sun was out so we drove to the beach.

We walked down cement stairs and along a sea wall. We walked along the beach looking for an empty space. The beach was shorter in length than I was used to. The people on the beach were sectioned off from each other in groups. They roped off a section of the sand from the wall to the ocean.

They looked like they were planning to stay a week with all the junk they had spread out: they had big umbrellas and tents, lawn chairs and kiddie pools, heavy-duty shovels for foxholes and bunkers, buckets, and sun hats, and radios, and ice chests, and four types of sun lotion. We tripped over sand sculptures and kids buried in the sand. Even the graffiti on the sea wall had family values to it. I could read what it said. "Billy loves Jean" and "Mike loves Nicole" and "Rock On." They were innocent.

We found a spot down the beach and laid our towels down. Scarlet wanted to go into the ocean. I went with her. The water was freezing. I ran back to the warmth of my towel. Cassidy was doing cartwheels. I asked Delilah if she wanted to get something to eat. We walked to the hamburger stand.

We ordered hamburgers as the sun disappeared. We got ice cream and Delilah fed me. We held hands and walked down the beach in silence. We saw Jesus sunbathing.

Scarlet found a party that night. We stopped at a gas station for booze. She gave me a list of beer to buy for her friends. I was tired of buying beer for everyone.

"Did it ever occur to you to ask me first?" I said.

"What for?" asked Scarlet.

"To be polite."

"Well, I am asking you now, it's no big deal, I made a list."

"You just assume I'll do it."

"Fine, I won't ask you again."

"Great."

"I can't go in with you." Scarlet said, as we pulled into the liquor store parking lot.

"You expect me to carry this all myself?"

"I went to school with the girl behind the counter."

"So what?"

"She knows I'm not old enough."

"I'm the only one buying it."

"Yeah, but in New Hampshire, everyone must be of age."

"What's the problem?"

"You're the problem."

"What are you getting mad at me for?"

"I'm buying all your friends beer and getting stuck paying for it."

"Why didn't you tell me you needed money?"

"Whatever. It's not important. Forget it." I got out of the Jeep and went inside to get the beer. I grabbed five cases out of the cooler and put them on the counter.

"Why don't you just buy a keg?" the cashier asked.

"Because my ex-girlfriend is hiding in the car and didn't want a keg."

"I was wondering why Scarlet was in the car. I went to high school with her."

"I know. She's hiding from you."

"Why?"

"Because she's an idiot."

"She was always a little strange."

"I know."

"It would be a lot easier if you got a keg."

"I know."

She rang up the beer and never asked for my license. The money Scarlet had given me was short but I had expected it. I made two trips to the car, while Scarlet hid. We brought the beer back to the party. I took a few beers and sat in the Jeep alone.

CHAPTER 8

The next day, Scarlet's mom made me waffles. Scarlet didn't want me talking to her mom. She pulled me away to another room.

"What were you doing?" she demanded.

"I was eating waffles. You told me to eat."

"Exactly. Who told you to be friends with her?"

"You did. You're the one who wanted us to meet her."

"Well, I didn't want you to become best friends with her."

"Don't you understand? We had a bonding moment. That doesn't happen all the time to me."

"She's playing with you. You can't trust her."

"I can't trust you either. What the hell do you want from me?"

I went outside. The Chief was peeling a Grateful Dead sticker off the back of Scarlet's car.

"You know this is an automatic pull-over," he said, not looking at me.

"What's that?" I asked.

"These rock group stickers here on the back."

"Oh, yeah?"

"Cops hate hippies."

I wondered if the cops hated his daughter as much as I did. "I'm beginning to see why," I mumbled.

Scarlet and her mom spilled out the front door arguing. "Tell your daughter that she is not going to Vermont."

"I'm staying out of this one," said the Chief.

"Do you know what they do up there?"

"It's a music festival, Mom. What's the big deal?" said Scarlet.

"It's a drug festival is what it is. You're grounded."

"You're being so unfair."

"Well, that's too bad because you are not going." Her mom stormed inside. We were left with the Chief.

"Just get in the car and go," he said to Scarlet, "I'll take care of your mother."

"Are you sure, Dad?"

"Just go."

"Thanks, I love you."

"Get out of here."

We drove off. Scarlet's mom ran out, yelling at the Chief. I smiled and waved.

We entered Vermont, descending into a valley of light fog that chased away the afternoon sun. Jesus was standing in the middle of the road staring at the sky. Scarlet pulled up next to him, but he didn't notice us.

"What's the deal with this Jesus guy?" Anna asked. "He's everywhere."

"He's got money in his hand," said Scarlet.

"And some tickets," said Delilah.

"This guy is so high right now."

Scarlet took a ticket from his right hand and put five dollars in his left hand.

We rolled down a hill until we arrived in a giant field next to a river. We parked the Jeep in the middle of the field and jumped out to stretch. I put the tailgate down and opened a beer.

The Grateful Dead was playing on the top of a hill. Scarlet ran off and came back with three big balloons of nitrous. She began to inhale and exhale. I could almost hear the waah-wah-waa-wah numbing effects of the nitrous. She lost her mind.

The sun was setting. We hurried to the band playing on a hillside. The Grateful Dead was playing "Fire on the Mountain," my favorite song, but I was miserable. I turned around and walked back to the Jeep.

Delilah followed me. "What's wrong?" she asked.

"I don't want to be here," I said.

"Do you want to talk about it?"

"No, I just want to get drunk. I was supposed to be with Scarlet on the hillside enjoying our favorite band but she doesn't care about me."

"She's not going to change. She's not going to love you."

"I know."

"You can't force her to love you."

"I know." I opened a beer.

"People don't change. She won't change."

"I know."

"You're in love with the idea of being in love with her." Delilah kissed me. It was a pity kiss, but I needed it.

The girls came back to the car just as the last star lit up the sky. The smell of smoke from bonfires filled the air. The girls took off their clothes and ran through the night naked. I stayed by the Jeep. It rained. The ground was wet. I crawled into my sleeping bag. Sleep was the only comfort I had left. I watched Jesus dragging his cross along the tree line in the distance.

CHAPTER 9

It rained through the night. I stepped out of the Jeep into mud. My body ached. Delilah heard me moan.

"Are you alright?" Delilah laughed. I loved her laugh.

"Nothing a drink won't take care of," I said.

"It's six in the morning."

"Oh, then I'd better have two."

"I guess I have no other excuse than to have one with you."

"A woman after my own heart." I handed her a beer.

Cassidy woke up next with a horrible cough. She got out of the Jeep and threw up. She came back looking green. "I want to leave," Cassidy said, spitting out the window.

"Fine with me but the monster is still asleep." I whispered.

"I'll drive and she can sleep," said Anna, sitting up.

"You don't have any insurance for this car," said Scarlet, sticking her head up.

"Do you want to drive right now?" asked Anna.

"No, I want to sleep," said Scarlet.

"So shut up and give me the keys."

"Just be careful driving."

"Just go back to sleep."

Anna took the wheel. She had a motherly instinct. We quietly slipped out of the valley in the early morning. We drove past the small towns and waved goodbye to the cows in the pastures. Delilah had fallen asleep on my shoulder. I slowly drank beer and stared out the window. My legs fell asleep. They were wedged between a gallon of water and some books. I didn't want to move in case I woke Delilah.

We went to the Elvis Café that night.

"It looks like the landing zone for the unemployed," whispered Anna. It was an open mic night. There was supposed to be a comet storm.

I got up on stage. Scarlet begged me not to. I grabbed the microphone and adjusted it, waving off Scarlet. "Here's a little poem for all you girls out there."

Delilah and Anna cheered like devoted groupies.

"The comets are coming. The comets are coming. Flip flop, flip flop, girls like to shop. There's a comet up there and we're stuck down here. The dreamers look up and stare, but the girls don't care. They are too worried about their hair. Thank you." I took a bow. Anna and Delilah cheered again.

We didn't stay long because Scarlet was sure the place was going to get raided by the cops. Her father had told her to stay away.

We went home. The girls fell asleep in front of the TV. I snuck outside to watch the comet shower. A shooting star fell brightly over the front yard. It was so close I could have caught it. Millions of stars painted into the universe. It was almost heaven. I heard a scraping sound coming from the street. I walked down the driveway to the road. Jesus appeared, carrying a wooden cross. He stopped a few feet in front of me.

"Can you give me a hand?" he asked.

"Sure. Didn't I see you in Vermont yesterday?"

"You know, there's an old Eskimo legend that says they aren't stars but merely openings where our loved ones choose to shine down on us."

"Who are you?" I asked.

"I'm Jesus."

"Really?"

"My friends call me JC." A peacefulness came over me.

"I've seen you before," I said.

"Yes, I've been with you the whole trip."

"I saw you in Boston. On the street and at the concert by the river."

"A few other places."

"Is this Christophany? The manifestation of Christ?"

"It's more like pareidolia."

"What are you doing here?" I asked.

"It's time to go home."

"Right now?"

"Yes, she doesn't love you."

"I just thought she would change."

"The only people who change are in movies."

"How will I heal from this?"

"You won't, but time moves us on. There's nothing here for you. I know you love her, but it's over." JC motioned for me to go inside. I hurried upstairs and grabbed my things. Scarlet stopped me by the front door.

"Where are you going?" she asked.

"To the airport."

She knew I was serious. "Let me drive you."

We drove in silence for the last time. Scarlet stopped the Jeep and got out with me.

I set my bag down and looked Scarlet. I had finally stopped being weak. She felt like a stranger.

"I love you," I said.

"What?"

"You heard me."

Her lips trembled. "How can you say that after the way I've treated you?"

"I mean it." I didn't, though. It was the meanest thing I could think of.

"Will you ever forgive me?" The shock on her face was enough satisfaction.

"No."

"Why the hell did you stay so long?"

"I was in love with you."

"I wish I never met you."

"I know." I let go. She grabbed hold of my arm.

"Wait," she whispered.

I turned and walked away.

CHAPTER 10

My respect for authority was quickly fading after last night's events. It was all behind me, and I looked forward to Halloween weekend in Isla Vista. I was tired, but sleep was out of the question. What sounded really nice was a cold beer.

"One pack of non-filter Camel cigarettes," said the deputy. "A pair of dice and Fruit Stripe gum. Two condoms and a Santa Claus PEZ dispenser. One bottle of prescription pills and a wallet with fifteen dollars, three arcade tokens, an expired Visa card, UCSB school identification, and a picture of Richard Nixon."

The door buzzed. I stepped out to freedom. The sky was overcast. I fished my sunglasses out of my jacket. A cab pulled up and I got in.

I had spent the better part of the night in jail for resisting arrest. I was completely innocent.

It started the night before with a couple of drinks near Cal Poly San Luis Obispo University with a foreign exchange student named Figgy. He was from Finland. I met Figgy for a beer.

When the bars closed, Figgy and I ate some mushrooms. I was on the handlebars of his bike when we crashed into a tree. Figgy managed to keep the bike straight and we got home.

"Why didn't we just drive?" I asked.

"No can do, my friend," said Figgy. "Too many crazy drunks out on the roads these days. You've got to watch out for yourself."

"Where'd you get this bike, anyway?" I asked.

"I got it from that rack outside the bar."

"You mean you stole it?" I asked.

"No, I borrowed it. There is a difference. I just don't intend to return it."

"Well, at least you didn't steal it. That's the important part."

When we got to the driveway of Figgy's apartment, we took a sharp right and smashed into a carload of girls. I landed on the hood. Figgy was on the ground, moaning. I stumbled over to him.

"We're home!" I exclaimed, trying to cheer myself up.

"I think I dislocated my shoulder!" screamed Figgy.

"Well, you're lucky to be in America," I said. "We have top notch medical care in this country."

"Are you guys all right?" asked the girl driving the car.

"Oh, yeah," I said. "We do this all the time. Don't worry about us."

"You scared the hell out of us," she said with a laugh. "We're all on mushrooms, and that really tripped us out."

"Good for you," I said. "More people should be on mushrooms. What are you girls doing tonight?"

"We're going to get some beer before the store closes. It's almost two."

"Great. Come on over when you get back. Do you know where this guy lives?" I pointed at Figgy.

"I live next door to Figgy," the girl said. "I think you should get him to the hospital. It looks like he broke his arm or something."

"He'll be fine. Nothing a few cocktails can't fix."

Figgy pulled himself up and leaned over the hood of the car. I picked up the bike and checked it for any damage. The front tire was bent. It was useless. I tossed it in some bushes.

"How's my car?" she asked.

The middle of the hood had a dent.

"Everything's fine," I assured her.

Figgy let out a warrior's cry and smashed his shoulder against the hood of the car. His shoulder made a cracking sound that echoed through the night. The cracking of bones was followed by a pop as his shoulder slide back into place. The girls in the car screamed.

"That was the coolest thing I've ever seen in my entire life," I said.

"I think I'm going to puke," groaned Figgy. His face was purple.

"I've got to get this guy upstairs," I said, turning toward the girls, "and administer some pain killers."

"We'll be over later," the girl said, taking a drag of her cigarette.

"Don't bother!" cried Figgy.

I grabbed Figgy and pulled him up the stairs to his apartment. We went inside.

Figgy went straight to the icebox and tossed me a beer. "Nothing like a cold soldier after a traffic collision," he said.

Figgy and I sat on the couch and drank. After he passed out, I wrote my name on his forehead with a marker. I wanted Figgy to get the full American college experience.

An hour later the campus police showed up. They were looking for Figgy. He was passed out under the coffee table. They didn't see him. Figgy was wanted by Interpol. You just never really know someone. The cop saw a bong on top of the coffee table and grabbed it.

"This looks like an apparatus for smoking the illegal substance known as marijuana," he said.

He arrested me, convinced that I was Figgy. I tried to explain who I was but the cop had tunnel vision. He locked me up with the rest of the rapists, crackheads, killers, and degenerates. I didn't like jail.

"What are you in for?" asked a man with no teeth. He shadowboxed against the wall.

"Jaywalking," I said. "What about you?"

"I burned down a church. But it wasn't me."

"Of course it wasn't," I said. "Who was it?"

"The CIA. They planted a chip in my skull."

"I know what you mean."

He stopped shadowboxing.

"Do you have one too?" he asked.

"I used to, but they took it out, because the microwave in the coffee room wasn't working."

"They got my chip out of a toaster before they put it in my brain."

"Those bastards," I said.

"Shh. There it is. Do you hear it? Can you hear the chip buzzing in my head?"

"I think so," I said. "What are they saying?"

"They're speaking in Russian. I can't decode the message."

"Damn it. I can only translate Chinese. Keep trying. Use your decoder ring if you have to."

"Good idea," he said. He banged his head against the wall and then dropped to the floor crying. He took his socks off and jammed them into the toilet. Water flooded the floor as he repeatedly flushed.

"Does this have something to do with the CIA?" I asked.

"No. It's just a lot of fun," he giggled.

"I see. Why exactly are you doing that?" I asked.

"You've got to make them work for a living."

"Who's that?"

"The pigs, man. If they throw you in here, you've got to make them pay!"

The holding cell looked like a swimming pool.

"Which one of you bastards did this?" a deputy demanded at the door.

"It was him," said the guy with no teeth, pointing at me.

"I should have known it was the punk college kid," said the deputy.

"Don't look at me," I said. "The CIA made me do it."

"Well, have a nice breakfast, shit heads!"

"Thanks. We will," said No Teeth, laughing. The deputy left.

"Are you going to eat your breakfast?" No Teeth asked.

"No, I'm not very hungry," I said.

"And your toast?" he asked.

"Take it all," I said.

"When someone does me a solid, I don't forget it."

"It's just breakfast," I said.

"You're my best friend. Let's hook up after we get out of here."

"Sure," I said. "My name is Figgy."

They released me in the morning. No charges. No court. Just a waste of time. I was anxious to get back to Isla Vista. Halloween was like Christmas for me. It was the biggest event in Santa Barbara. A hundred thousand people had shown up last year to walk the streets of Del Playa. *Playboy Magazine* had voted Isla Vista the greatest place in the world to party. The streets were so jammed with people that there was barely any room to stand.

CHAPTER 11

I found my car at Figgy's place. JC jumped in just as I was about to leave. I hadn't been able to shake him since New Hampshire.

"Where we going?" asked JC.

"I'm going to Isla Vista," I said. "Are you ready?"

"You bet," JC said excitedly.

"Let's roll."

I pulled out onto the street and found the 101 Highway heading south. JC turned up the radio. We were homeward bound with the wind whipping through our hair and cold soldiers in our hands. JC flipped open the ashtray and pulled out half a joint.

"Let's light this baby up," JC said.

I smiled. "This day is getting better by the minute."

I lit the joint and checked the rearview mirror for any cops lingering in the background. The sweet smell of dope filled the car. JC flicked the roach out the window when he was done and slumped back into his seat.

There was a McDonald's on the outskirts of San Luis Obispo. I veered off the highway. We flew down the off-ramp and parked in a green zone across the street from the McDonald's. I set my watch for fifteen minutes.

"Maybe if you hadn't taken your sweet time back at Figgy's place, watching that *Land of the Lost* marathon, you wouldn't be in a hurry."

"We have plenty of time," I said.

McDonald's was packed. I took my place in line behind the rest of the zombies. I chose the line that was farthest from the door. It appeared to have fewer people in it. Four people stood in front of me. They stared at a blonde two rows over in a tight red dress. She looked like Marilyn Monroe. I focused my attention to my left, where three people sat on a bench, waiting for their orders. A man leaned against the wall, laughing to himself. A tiny man with glasses, who appeared to be Woody Allen, waited on a bench.

I glanced down at my watch and noticed that five minutes had gone by. The blonde in the tight red dress was gone. My line hadn't moved. I looked behind me to see if anyone else had noticed. A huge pig-man towered over me. I was certain that he was a cop. He'd been tailing me. He was going to jump me right after he got his food. I was sure of it.

It was getting hot. I could feel sweat dripping off my brow. I brought my shoulders up to my neck and stood with my arms crossed. I could hear Woody Allen complaining about his order.

"This is crazy," said Woody. "I ordered my food a half hour ago."

"Yes, sir," said the cashier, "but you ordered something special, and that takes longer than the other orders."

"All I ordered was a plain hamburger," said Woody. "This is crazy. I mean, my Lord, how long does it take for a plain hamburger?"

"Just a few more minutes."

Woody stammered. "I—it's just crazy."

The cashier was slow. She resembled a bumblebee.

"Must be new," said JC, who popped up behind me.

"She doesn't even know how to use the cash register."

The lights bounced off the metal counters. I had five minutes left until the parking meter expired. The line moved up two people. A man who looked like Albert Einstein ran out of patience. He switched lines just in time and caught a flow up to the front. I watched as he ordered his food without hesitation.

"You should have switched lines when you had the chance," said JC.

Woody Allen finally got his plain hamburger. He felt the need to explain to the Bumblebee, in detail, how upset he was.

"I'm in a rush, and I need to get to work," said Woody. "This is crazy."

"That's nice," said the Bumblebee.

"I don't like to complain, but if I'm late, they'll fire me."

"That's nice," said the Bumblebee.

"I mean, I like this place," said Woody. "I come here a lot, but I can't be late for work. Do you understand?"

Two old women giggled behind him. They looked like Lucy and Ethel.

"What are you going to get?" Ethel asked.

"Oh, I just don't know," Lucy said.

"Are you going to get the apple pie?" asked Ethel.

"Heavens no! Those just go straight to my hips."

"So, what are you going to get?"

"I can't make up my mind," said Lucy. "Something without fat."

"I'm on a diet too," said Ethel.

"Three minutes," whispered JC.

The Bumblebee asked Lucy and Ethel what they wanted as the cop behind me stormed out.

"I'll take a Big Mac, fries, large Coke, and an apple pie," Lucy said.

"What about the hips?" asked Ethel.

"What the heck," Lucy said with a smile. "You only live once."

"Oh, heavens to Betsy, you're a wild one." Ethel turned to me, smiling as if she'd just said the funniest thing in the whole world.

I lost my appetite and ran to my car. I cracked an amyl under my nose as JC turned up the radio full volume.

I drove off. I highly recommended putting on "Peace Frog" by the Doors at ear-piercing decibels.

"You'd better slow down," said JC.

"What for?" I asked. "We're making great time."

"We just passed a Chippy," said JC.

"What? Where?" I asked.

"That was a speed trap back there."

"A cop?" I asked, still not believing him. I caught a glimpse of the cop car coming through a dust cloud.

"You'd better pull over," said JC.

"Can't you work some magic?"

"I don't do traffic stops."

I flew past the next off ramp.

"You missed the off ramp!" cried JC.

I jerked the wheel into some hedges.

I turned off the car off and waited. The silence seemed to last forever until I heard an engine racing towards us. We watched the cop fly by with sirens blaring.

JC smiled. "You just created a miracle."

We waited awhile, then eased onto the highway homeward bound.

CHAPTER 12

I knew everything would be fine once I abandoned my car.

"Most accidents happen within a mile of your home," said JC. I parked on the street and ran inside my house to safety. I placed my beer in the icebox and sat down on the couch.

The People's Court was on TV. My roommate Shakes drank Jack Daniel's and filled in a crossword puzzle. We called him "Shakes" because he was such an alcoholic.

"What's going on?" I asked.

"You've got to check out this *People's Court*. This girl is suing her mom for two grand. The mother promised her daughter two grand if she didn't get into trouble, do drugs, or have sex before she was 21. Now the mom won't pay up."

"If the girl really did all that, she's got to be plain stupid," I said.

"She sure looks like she wouldn't have any problem pulling it off."

"I wouldn't have done it for all the money in the world."

"The mom should've lobotomized her instead."

I had five roommates, but Shakes was the only one I spoke to. Broken glass and burnt telephone books littered the floor. Stapled to the walls were candy wrappers, hung like trophies. Scattered on the walls were spackle marks from holes made by randoms. Someone had spray painted a monster on the wall in the hallway. An axe stuck in its head. They called it art.

We had six televisions, one with a baseball bat sticking out. The house had flooded. We used skateboards to get from room to room. Everyone just assumed that someone else had called the plumber. Any outsider would have thought the place was a regular crack house. Most of the furniture had been burned in a drunken stupor. I was positive a certain smell was from a wild animal that had crawled into the place and died. Random people appeared every evening to party, except on Sundays, because everyone wanted to sleep.

I took another hit of acid and sat on the couch for an hour. I had a great head trip. I was in Greece, with a flamenco guitar softly playing in my head. My peaceful vacation was interrupted by Shakes.

"I took a nitrous tank from my dad's office. It's in my car. Nothing is more enticing than being in the clutches of free nitrous."

We parked the car under a shady oak tree. I don't know why we left the house, but it had seemed like the right thing to do. We sat back inhaling our balloons as the strange and distorted boxed figures danced in our brains.

No one noticed that the car was rolling or that it jumped a curb onto the front lawn of a house. Shakes had left the car in neutral.

"What are you doing?" I asked Shakes.

"What a beautiful garden," he replied. Shakes was slumped over the wheel. The owners of the house looked out the window. I waved. I grabbed Shakes. His eyes shot open.

"What did I do?" he asked.

"You might want to put the car in reverse and get off these people's lawn," I replied calmly.

He punched the car into reverse and peeled out.

"You can slow down now," I said when we were a good distance away.

"I think the nitrous tank leaked."

Shakes had mass paranoia running through his brain and didn't slow down until we got back home. We hid the car in the garage and checked it for damage.

"Bad karma, my friends," Shakes said. "We don't need anything else like that happening this weekend. Let's take the tank inside."

"That sounds like a smart idea," I said.

"I think you need to slow down," said JC.

"I think you may be right," I agreed.

The neighbors came over with some hash. I just couldn't refuse the smell of hash. A few hits made me realize that there was no time to relax. I needed to get some more beer. I dashed out the front door.

At the nearest liquor store I bought beer and vodka.

"You've got to stop drinking," insisted JC.

"How can I when there's a liquor store on every corner in Isla Vista?"

"Willpower."

"I don't have any."

"I'll give you some." JC put me in a head lock. I was powerless holding the alcohol. We struggled outside.

"Let go," I whined.

Shakes appeared and grabbed the beer.

"What are you doing?" asked Shakes.

"I was wrestling with JC."

Shakes gave me a strange look. "I hate to tell you, but you were beating yourself up."

JC was gone. I sat on the ground with my arms locked around my chest.

"I think you need to take it easy for the rest of the night," said Shakes.

"That's what JC told me," I said.

"You're not talking about your imaginary friend again, are you?"

"He was just here..." I shook my head. "It doesn't matter. What are you doing here, anyway?"

"I ran out of smokes. I was on my way to get some when I saw you wrestling with yourself in the street."

"I thought you were trying to quit. That only lasted about five hours." I handed Shakes a cigarette.

"Are you sure you're okay?" asked Shakes.

"Yeah, the ground broke my fall."

CHAPTER 13

A party had materialized in our living room when I got back. The music thumped through the walls. I tried to sleep but people banged on my bedroom door trying to get me to join them.

I was so annoyed that I tossed an M-80 out the door to quiet the party. It only seemed to excite them. The party got louder.

JC woke me around midnight to go downtown. I slowly dressed. I felt like a zombie. The nap didn't help. I downed some speed with a cup of coffee and set out for the night. I figured I could at least get half the sleep I needed while driving if I kept one eye closed.

The house was packed. I couldn't get to the door without someone stopping me.

"Where are you going?" asked Shakes.

"I've got to go downtown," I said.

"What for?" he asked.

"They've nominated me for the Nobel Peace Prize," I said.

"Come on. Stay and party with us."

"I'll be back in about an hour," I said.

"Okay. Then we'll drink a few when you get back?"

"You got it."

"Will you sign my petition before you go?" he asked.

"What's it for?"

"It's to legalize drugs."

"Are you insane?" I asked. I shuffled to a corner of the room.

"What's wrong?" he shot back.

"You'll be put on a government watch list."

"That's crazy."

"Don't you get it? Not to make you paranoid or anything, but the government is watching us. Just because you're in college doesn't mean you have freedom. Save a tree or something but don't ever sign a petition."

JC and I walked out to my car and jumped in. I opened the glove box and pulled out a pack of Zig-Zags to roll a joint.

"This is empty," I said. "Where are the papers?"

"You're out," said JC. "Let's go get some at the store."

"Can't you make one out of thin air?"

"I can only make water into wine."

"Well, what else could we use? Check the glove box again."

"All you've got in here is an autographed baseball card of Steve Howe."

"Give it to me," I said.

We were just about to roll one with the baseball card when JC remembered that there were still some beers in the back. He shot-gunned a beer and then poked some holes in the top of the beer can.

"Maybe if you had a pipe we wouldn't have to sit around thinking up ways to get stoned," I said.

"Maybe if you had a brain," said JC, "you'd remember to bring one yourself."

I started the car, and we rolled into the night toward the freeway.

"If I saw someone walking backwards, naked, juggling, with a ten-foot python around his neck, I wouldn't even blink," I told JC.

"It's the nature of the beast, and the beast is Isla Vista," he said. Only someone from out of town would think there was a need to call the police. The town existed off the freaks randomly lingering around.

When we got to Los Carneros Street, JC spotted a bum holding a sign that read, "WHY LIE? I NEED A BEER." I reached in the back seat and tossed him a cold soldier out of the sunroof.

"God bless you, my friend!" the bum hollered.

"No, God bless you!" I yelled back.

"That was nice of you," said JC.

"I know," I said.

"I would have thought you'd rather give him money than your last beer."

"People change," I said.

"Things change. People just stay the same."

"It feels good to give a little back to the community," I said. I was suddenly struck by a dark feeling of loneliness. I couldn't shake it. Ideas began to throng my mind. I concluded that all the problems of society were artificial. I couldn't fix them.

A light drizzle came down on the empty highway. I tapped the wipers.

"Did I ever tell you about the time I found a mouse in a beer bottle?" said JC.

"That was me who found the mouse in the beer bottle!" I said.

"I was there too," said JC.

"No one else believes me but you."

"Have you ever heard how Halloween came to be?"

"Only from the makers of fine candy."

"Well, it means 'holy or hallowed evening'. It was named after the day before All Saints' Day and was an early pagan festival. The wacky heathen costumes soon followed. It was the end of summer, and the beginning of winter. It was the

Celts' New Year's celebration in what's now France and the British Isles. The Druid priests performed mystic ceremonies to the great Sun God at a place we all know as Stonehenge."

"In England?" I asked.

"Oh, so you know the story?" asked JC.

"No, I'm just wondering where you heard it."

"On the Discovery Channel, of course. Now let me continue."

"Go ahead," I said.

"It was at these autumn festivals that the Druids tried to placate the Lord of Death. It was to allow the spirits of those who died in the past year to spend a few hours at their homes. They lit bonfires on hilltops to frighten away the evil spirits."

"And to honor the Sun God," I said.

"Exactly. People would sing and dance around the fires, pretending to be pursued by evil spirits. It was a time where myths and fairytales were facts, and witches rode on broomsticks. The women sold themselves to the Devil, and in return, he let them ride over the pale moon. Ghosts and goblins played tricks on humans. It was a time when black cats, werewolves, bats, fairies, pixies, and freaks roamed the earth."

"Global warming killed them off," I said.

"The priests would cut up animals and they could tell the future by the insides."

"What about bobbing for apples?" I asked.

"The Romans honored the Goddess of Fruit, and that's where they got bobbing for apples. People would throw apple peels over their shoulders to foresee their mates. And eating a piece of bread before going to sleep meant any wish would come true. The jack-o'-lantern is said to have originated from an Irishman named Jack who loved to play pranks on the Devil."

"What a cool guy," I said.

"Jack was condemned to wander the earth, carrying a lantern to light his way. They didn't have flashlights back then."

"No shit? So, what about all that trick or treat jazz?" I asked.

"That's all from the United States. The taffy pulls, corn popping, and hayrides were first, and then came the pranks. Like taking off gates to let cows and pigs run loose."

"Those crazy kids," I said.

"Other pranks were to change the numbers on houses or street signs."

"Now they cruise the streets in creepy vans. Or hand out cyanide-covered candy bars stuffed with razor blades." I said.

"And they all show up in Isla Vista to run wild down Del Playa," said JC.

"Only in America!" I said. We got off the freeway and made our way to a warehouse on Ortega Street. I parked the car and fished through my pockets for a hit of Ecstasy.

"What did you take that for?" asked JC.

"My doctor prescribed it and we're going to a rave. When you go to a rave, you take Molly."

"Not everyone at a rave is on something," said JC.

"Then why did you bring me here?"

"You'll see."

There was a line at the door. I followed JC. The line parted like the Red Sea. We got inside and took an elevator upstairs. The bottom floor was decorated to look like Hell. The floor was sticky.

The top floor was Heaven. It smelled like cotton candy. The doors opened and JC pointed to Delilah. She was stunning. She threw her arms around me.

"Why did you leave me in New Hampshire?" Delilah asked.

"I'm sorry. I thought you'd understand."

"I get it. You had to get over her. I'm divorced now."

"I've never stopped thinking about you."

"I know."

"Do you want to take some Molly with me?"

"Hell yes."

There is no final stopping point when you're on ecstasy. You are torn between your uncontrolled desires. I was in a state of bliss and craved more of it. I felt like I was going to explode. Delilah was keeping me together. I held her like she had died and been resurrected.

JC interrupted us. "Time to go."

"We just got here," I said. It had been an hour but felt like seconds.

"The cops are about to bust this place. Trust me. You'll see her later."

I kissed Delilah and dashed out of the warehouse.

CHAPTER 14

It was morning. I fished through the glove box for my sunglasses. It took me a while to find them. I didn't notice that JC was wearing them.

"I've got to keep my head in place before it explodes," I said.

"Here's a Steelers football helmet," said JC.

I donned the Steelers helmet. We drove home. I turned left on Carrillo Street and bumped into a car sitting at a red light.

"All I was trying to do was get on the freeway," I said.

"Act normal," said JC.

"Can I do that?" I asked.

"Be polite and pray that there isn't any damage."

"Be polite? Act normal?" I repeated.

A bald man wobbled out of a rusty blue Toyota Celica, scratching his head.

"I'm sorry, sir. Are you all, right?" I asked.

"Huh?" he mumbled.

"You gave him brain damage!" shouted JC.

"I guess I'm all right," the man said as he checked the rear bumper for damage.

"Say something to him!" shouted JC.

"What do you want me to say?" I mumbled.

"Keep him busy. Old people love to talk," said JC.

"Are you sure you're all right, sir?" I asked again.

"Well, I guess so, young feller," said the old man. "No harm, no foul."

"I totally agree with you, sir," I said.

"No sense in making a big hoopla out of the whole thing."

"Thank you very much, sir. You have yourself a nice day." I turned around and put one foot in the door.

The old man called after me. "What's with the helmet you got there on your head, son?"

"You look like an idiot," said JC.

"I've got practice up at Harder Stadium. The team's waiting for me."

"I played a little ball back in my day too," he said. "What position do you play?"

"Quarterback. The name's Bradshaw. Terry Bradshaw Jr."

"Well, I'll be darned. It's an honor, Mr. Bradshaw."

"Please, call me Terry," I said. I jumped back in the car and gunned it to the freeway. I barreled onto the 217 freeway until I hit a traffic jam.

"What's with the traffic?" asked JC.

"There must be an accident," I said.

"The cops are checking for residents."

"I don't have any proof," I said.

"All you have is this toy cop badge," said JC.

"Hand it to me."

"You're insane! What are you going to do?"

I held up the toy badge. We breezed through the checkpoint. I winked at JC and then noticed a campus cop hiding behind a tall hedge in his cruiser. Campus cops were twice as dumb as normal cops. The cop rolled out behind me. I pulled into the parking lot across from Phelps Hall.

I made a quick check of the car and put my hands at ten and two on the steering wheel. I leaned my head back and tried to shake off the trailers looming in my brain.

"How are doing today?" asked the cop.

"Fine," I said. "Did I do something wrong, officer?"

"Like he's never heard that one before," said JC.

"Shut up," I mumbled.

"Did you just tell me to shut up?" asked the cop.

"No," I said, 'Sun's up.' It's a gorgeous day out, officer. Don't you think?"

"Can I see your license and registration?"

"I'm awfully sorry about that. I guess I got a little carried away and took those turns a little too fast."

"You were going 10 miles an hour," the cop said.

"Well, you can never be too safe. I thought the speed limit was 10 miles an hour."

"It's a 25 zone," he said. "The 10-mile sign is for hospital zones."

"I'll remember that next time. Just trying to be extra cautious this weekend. I read that there are a lot of outta-towners coming here and causing trouble."

"Are you a resident of Isla Vista?" he asked.

"To be honest, I can't get away from the place. It kind of sucks you in."

"I know exactly what you mean. You wouldn't happen to have some registration or other proof that this vehicle is yours?"

"Didn't I hand it to you with my license?" I asked.

"No, you handed me a prayer card."

"I seem to have misplaced it," I said.

"Did you know that your license expired a month ago?"

"Yeah, I was just on my way to take care of that after I went home and changed my clothes. I just got off work. I'm a security guard," I blurted out. I held up the badge, but that didn't seem to impress him. He turned his head and scoffed.

"The tattoo of Porky Pig on his arm gives him a sense of irony," said JC.

"Okay, I'm going to make you a deal," said the cop. "I'm going to give you a warning for the speed and registration. Then I'll write you a ticket for not wearing your seat belt."

"Not wearing my seat belt?" I asked.

"That way, we both get what we want, and we can enjoy the rest of the day. You can just pay the fine by mail." He handed me the ticket. I felt mentally assaulted.

I was bitter as I drove off. I was wearing my seat belt.

"Cops out here just making stuff up," laughed JC.

"Frightening and yet slightly amusing," I agreed.

We passed the information booth across from the Fountain Blue dorms. I spotted a shiny object in the distance. It was a keg!

"What are they doing over there?" JC asked.

"They're playing the greatest game ever, sloshball," I said.

Usually in the fourth inning, everyone is so drunk that no one can remember how to play the game. Batting styles frequently change throughout the game as the heavy-eyed players slouch over the plate, trying not to pass out. The pitcher directs every pitch at the batter's head because it's the only thing he can make out from such a distance. Your own teammates heckle you and degrade your ancestors. The baseball glove has been replaced by another beer cup so as not to cause a line at the keg. The game is usually abandoned by intoxicated players who wander off the field in an alcoholic haze.

"Ty Cobb would have loved it," laughed JC.

"It's a fast-paced version of America," I said. "You gotta love sloshball."

I jerked the wheel to the right and jumped the curb. I drove the bike path as angry joggers screamed at me. The radio was so loud that I couldn't make out their profanities. I smiled and waved back.

I slammed on the brakes and came to a halt just a few feet from the keg. An angry mob surrounded the car.

"I figure I can at least get the keg tap in my mouth before they start beating me," I shouted to JC.

"At least you have a plan," JC said.

"What the hell, I have insurance."

"I think it's expired," said JC.

"It doesn't matter," I said.

I admit that driving your car into a crowd of people just to get a beer may sound insane, but it was Isla Vista.

I got the tap to my mouth as the shortstop charged me. Then a voice from the heavens shouted out and saved me.

"It's okay! I know this guy!" said the voice.

The voice was Crazy Eddie. He was an eighth-year junior with a tattoo of George Bush smoking crack on his neck. Crazy Eddie worked for a pharmaceutical company and always experimented with new drugs before they approved them. He was old. No one would mistake him for a college student.

"You interrupted our game," said Crazy Eddie.

"I was thirsty," I said.

"Move your car. We're in the middle of a game. And grab a mitt. We could use somebody on second."

"Great," I said. "I've got my own equipment in the trunk."

"To tell you the truth," said JC, "the guy makes me edgy, and hanging around with him gives me the creeps."

"You hit the nail on the head," I said.

I moved the car off the field. The game resumed with me standing at second base. I only played one inning. I was thrown out for spiking the shortstop. I hit a beautiful line drive to left field. The shortstop caught the ball just as I rounded first. I slid into his legs, and he fell back, hitting the edge of the keg. I got up and downed a beer.

"What the hell do you think you're doing?" demanded Crazy Eddie.

"I was trying to make it to second," I said.

"Bad play."

"He blocked the plate," I argued.

"Did you have to wear metal spikes?"

"It's a game, isn't it?" I said.

"I think you need to chill." Eddie took out a fistful of pills. "Take these."

"Isn't that, like, heroin?" I asked.

"Nonsense. It's completely different. Trust me."

"I don't believe him," said JC.

I took the pills. My legs gave out, and I fell over. Crazy Eddie picked me up and tossed me in the trunk of his old Camaro.

"Get that guy to the hospital!" someone shouted as Eddie slammed the trunk.

I lay dormant. My body felt numb. The only thing I could do was open one eye. My brain felt like a broken record. My mind and body were separated. I feared that they would never be connected again. I thought I would end up in a mental ward, with my friends watching me play checkers in a bathrobe.

"This guy is a hoodoo," said JC.

"I think I'm dying," I said. "What is a hoodoo?"

"It's something that brings bad luck," said JC.

Crazy Eddie stopped to pick up his girlfriend, Crazy Tina, in front of Java Jones Cafe. I felt sick. Crazy Tina got her name when the cops found her building a bird's nest on top of Stork Tower. To this day, no one knows how she got up there.

Eddie opened the trunk. Crazy Tina was startled by me. She screamed.

"I'm amazed someone with a name like 'Crazy Eddie' could even get a girlfriend," said JC.

Crazy Tina punched me.

"I'm walking home," Tina yelled. Crazy Tina stormed off.

"Now that you're awake, you might as well get in the car," said Crazy Eddie.

"Oh, no," I said. "I love the trunk. Let's drive around all fucking day!"

"Smart ass," said Crazy Eddie.

"Take me back to my car," I demanded.

"I need to return the keg," said Eddie.

We rolled over to the liquor store. I purchased two fifths of Captain Morgan's spiced rum, some Pixy Stix, and a pack of Camel non-filters.

Panic set over me when we returned to the baseball field. My car was gone. I went through the normal stages of loss. Losing a car in America is like losing a family member or a large dog. The car is an extension of the self.

"It's been stolen," I said.

"I don't think it was stolen," said Crazy Eddie. "It looks like a tow truck has been here."

"Then where's my car, Sherlock?" I asked.

"There's only one tow company in Isla Vista. Give 'em a call."

We drove to get my car. Crazy Eddie fished a bindle of coke out of his pocket and handed it to me. I looked at it for a few moments, pondering whether I should.

"Did you know that if you took all the bills in circulation and scraped them off, you'd have a hell of a lot of cocaine?" Eddie said.

"That's great," I said.

"In England, beer used to be a breakfast food."

"You mean it isn't anymore?" I asked.

"The average family spends nineteen hours a week in a tavern," said Crazy Eddie.

I snorted a line. I felt a burst of pain run through my head. I thought my brain was on fire. It was salt. Slayer played loudly. Crazy Eddie turned toward me with a goofy smile.

"It's good stuff," nodded Crazy Eddie.

"It's salt, you asshole!" I screamed.

"Yeah, I just got out of County for assault!"

"You need to go back there!" I yelled.

"I've got something in my hair?" Eddie asked.

"Do you have anything more?"

"Al Gore?"

"No," I said, turning down the radio and tossing the bindle out the window. "Do you have any more?"

"What, are you insane? That was fifty bucks of coke you just threw out the window!"

"I don't want you to become a drug addict," I joked.

Crazy Eddie grabbed my throat.

"It was salt!" I choked.

Eddie let go of my throat.

We found the tow yard. It was in a back alley. An industrial area of Goleta. Everything looked dead. A redneck leaning against a burned-out Chevy with a beer flagged us down.

"That must be him," I said.

"I've got the deuce-five locked and loaded," said Eddie holding up a gun.

"Put that thing away," I said.

"It's our backup," said Crazy Eddie.

"Just turn the car around, and let's get out of here," I said in a panic.

"I can't turn around in this alley," said Eddie. "It's too narrow."

"Might as well go on in. There's no turning back now."

We cruised through an electrical fence. I spotted my car sitting in the middle of an empty lot surrounded by dead weeds and chunks of broken glass. I was furious when I saw my car alone. It was like picking up your child from an abandoned day care.

"I'm Jimbo," said the redneck.

I turned to Crazy Eddie, "Just stay here for a few. Let me take care of things."

I stepped out of the car and followed Jimbo over to a dilapidated shed. A kid in a Batman costume jumped out from behind the shed. He kicked me.

"What is that?" I asked.

"That's just my boy," said Jimbo. "He's all dressed up to go egg some houses."

The kid nailed me in the chest with a handful of rocks.

"Momma is on medication," he sang.

The singing annoyed me, but I couldn't say anything. Jimbo picked up an ax and broke open a locked shed. He kicked open the shed door. He stepped inside and rummaged around. "I forgot my dang keys," he mumbled.

"How much did you say that was going to be?" I asked.

"That'll be 60 bucks," said Jimbo.

"I thought you said a hundred and forty?"

"Do you love America?" Jimbo asked.

"Yes."

"You just got ten more dollars knocked off your bill."

"He loves America," whispered JC.

I signed some papers and motioned to Crazy Eddie to follow me out. Jimbo opened the gate. My car roared with excitement. I turned on the radio and lit a cigarette. I felt like I was driving a new car. I headed down Hollister on my way back to Isla Vista. I made a mental note never to return to a tow yard. Crazy Eddie flagged me down at a red light.

"I shot myself in the leg!" he screamed. "I've got to get it checked out!"

"You did what?"

"I'll meet up with you later."

"Cool." I nodded. Crazy Eddie drove off. I continued down the road.

"What's going on?" JC asked.

"He shot himself in the leg," I said.

"What an idiot," said JC. "I don't know why they call him 'Crazy Eddie.' They should just call him 'Eddie Minus.'"

"How about just 'Dumbass'?" I laughed.

"That works too."

The adrenaline from the tow service encounter, mixed with the drugs, caused an overload in my body. I didn't even feel myself drifting off. It was as if someone hit me over the head with a cinder block. One second, I was happy as a clam, and the next second I was out for the count.

JC cracked an amyl under my nose and woke me up. "Here we go again," said JC. "There's a cop behind us."

I rolled down the window and took out my license.

"Could you turn off your engine, sir?" yelled the cop.

"Yeah, no problem," I responded.

"License and registration."

"Here ya go. Is there a problem?"

"I was just going to ask you that very question."

"Why's that?" I asked.

"Is there any reason why you're parked on the center divider?"

"I just had an asthma attack," I blurted. I showed him my bottle of prescription pills and coughed.

"My uncle died of asthma," said the cop. "That's some serious stuff."

"Don't I know it," I said, sighing in relief that he was buying it.

"Do you need any medical assistance?" he asked.

"No, I'm fine now," I said, popping a Ritalin in my mouth.

"Well, I'm not going to cite you for this, seeing how you have a medical condition, but next time be sure to take your pills before you get into your vehicle." He handed me back my license and registration.

"I will, officer, and thanks. You have a good day," I said.

The cop left. I took another Ritalin.

CHAPTER 15

I woke up on a couch. It was a good sleep. It was good to be off the streets. I didn't recognize anyone in the living room, but that was normal for Isla Vista. It was the only town where a stranger could be on your couch in the middle of the night and you didn't think anything of it.

The place looked cleaner. I guessed that a maid had been hired. The TVs were gone. There was only one chair, and it had a slipcover on it.

"Those bastards," I mumbled. I turned to a guy next to me. "Is this Pasado?"

"You mean, the street?" he asked.

"Yeah, is this 6690 Pasado?" I asked.

"No, that's next door."

"Do you know who lives here?" I asked.

"I do," he said.

"Then what am I doing here?" I asked.

"You stumbled in about an hour ago and passed out on the couch," he said.

"All these houses around here look the same," I said.

"Aren't you here for the meeting?"

"The meeting?" I asked.

"The Bible study meeting." My surroundings came into focus and I noticed the collared shirt and polished penny loafers. The snacks laid out on the coffee table next to the pitcher of Hawaiian Punch. Gospel music humming in the background. The smell of air freshener filling the room. I wondered what these people must have thought when I stumbled through the door wearing dark sunglasses, a beer-stained Reyn Spooner shirt, torn khaki shorts, and spiked baseball cleats.

"We're here to help you, Brother. You're among friends," he whispered.

"So you know Jesus?" I asked.

"Yes, and you need Jesus."

"I know Jesus."

"We're messengers of the Lord. We're here to help you with your sin."

"That's my best quality," I said. "Why would I want to get rid of that?"

"Surely you're not happy with your life?"

"I guess you're right," I said, standing up.

"We thought so. Now come sit down and pray with us, Brother."

"That's a wonderful idea. I just have to use the restroom, and then we'll work on stuff. Try to get all the sin out of me."

"Wonderful! The restroom is down the hall on the left. We'll pass around the peanut butter and celery sticks while we wait for you."

"That sounds swell," I said. I made my way to the restroom and locked the door. I fumbled with a tiny window above the shower. It appeared to be painted shut. I wrapped my hand in a towel and punched out the glass.

"Are you okay in there, Brother?" a voice asked.

I could hear people gathering in the hallway.

"Just fine!" I hollered back. "I'll be out in a second!" I tossed the towel over the windowsill and squirmed to freedom.

"What took you so long?" asked JC.

"Unlike you, I can't walk through walls and evaporate anytime I want to." I retorted. I ran to my house. "I'm home!" I shouted, stepping inside.

"Where have you been?" asked Shakes.

"I have no idea."

"We thought you got arrested."

"Impossible," I said.

"I made some homemade beer," said Shakes. "Just bottled a fresh batch. I've got some in that beer stein on the counter."

"Don't drink that," warned JC.

I went into the kitchen and drank a glass of beer. It seemed that in Isla Vista people were either making their own beer or growing their own weed. Shakes' beer was a bit lumpy, but I drank it down.

"What do you call this stuff?" I asked.

"GOGGLES. 'If she doesn't look good, then you need another.' Or something like that. That's gonna be the slogan. How do you like it?"

"One's enough for me. I think you need to brew it longer."

"Too strong?" he asked.

"No," I said. "It just tastes like crap."

"Wait a minute. Did you just drink out of Viking's mug?"

"Yeah, you told me to," I said.

"I told you to drink out of that beer stein," he said, pointing to a stein on the other side of the counter.

"What the hell did I just drink?" I asked.

"You just drank my psilocybin tea."

"What?" I asked. "You let me drink mushrooms?"

"You did it to yourself."

"How much did you put in there?" I asked.

"About an eighth."

"Great! I'm trying to slow down."

"I told you," said JC.

"Now I have someone to trip with," said Shakes.

"I'm glad you're happy," I said. "I'll just sit down on the couch and wait."

"That's fine. I'll be in the kitchen making another batch of GOGGLES beer."

I didn't feel anything for an hour, and thought Shakes was just fucking with me. I thought for sure he'd given me bogus mushrooms.

Then the shrooms kicked in. I couldn't focus on Shakes' face because he looked like a gigantic toad. His eyes were bigger than my head. When he talked, his tongue rolled a foot out of his mouth, like he was trying to eat a giant fly buzzing around the room. I thought he would zap me with his giant tongue and swallow me whole. I looked at my hand. Molecules were shooting out of my fingertips.

There was no way he could have possibly understood. I could see that he was disappointed that I didn't want another bong hit.

"It's an insult to decline a bong hit in some countries," JC whispered.

I carefully made my way into the hall, trying not to attract any attention. I stood in the hall for a few seconds and realized that I was acting too suspiciously. I made my way to the living room. A few more giant people had come over and were milling around the kitchen, watching Shakes brew his beer. They looked familiar. I was certain that I knew them, but I couldn't think of where I'd seen them before.

I tried to grab on to anything that seemed familiar. I sat down and put my feet up on the couch because the floor was moving. Pixies danced around me and tried to chew off my legs with their huge fangs. Pixies may be lovable and cute, but they can be vicious when you're high. I rolled up a magazine and tried my best to fend them off, but they were too fast for me. I sat in a frantic state, trying not to alert the others in the house to the danger that I'd lost my mind.

I separated myself. The thinker from the thought. The knower from the known. The subject from the object. Everything was purely abstract, and it scared me. There was nothing to grasp, and yet I struggled to grab on to an object. Any object of thought. I wanted to clutch it and hold on to it for dear life until the object meant something. I wanted it in my hands, so I could prove that it was a tangible thing. That I wasn't just imagining it. I looked around for JC. He was nowhere to be found. I was going to need stilts to walk over to the kitchen. It was the only safe place in the entire house. I'd have to make a break for it.

I sprang up off the couch, leaping into the kitchen.

"What the hell are you doing?" asked Shakes.

"I'm fine."

"You don't look so good."

"I feel great," I lied.

"Your face is ash. I mean, really ash looking."

"I'm great," I repeated.

"Do you feel sick?"

"Not me," I said. I figured if I told everyone that I was fine, I'd start to believe it myself. The only thing that I felt any attachment to was a Pittsburg Steelers mug on the counter.

"Did those mushrooms hit you?" asked Shakes.

"Nope," I said.

"You're about to be a Pass Out Victim," said Shakes.

I grabbed the mug and filled it with beer. I took a swig. It tasted bland. I was running out of oxygen. I threw the mug in the sink and took three steps backward. Then I turned around toward the kitchen again. It looked so far away.

I dashed out the front door and ran into the street. I tried to go home but I'd forgotten where I lived. I ran back to the driveway. My brain had detached itself. I was afraid it would never come back. I focused on my breathing. I could feel my breath touch my dry throat.

"Jack, what the hell are you doing in the middle of the street?" yelled Shakes.

"Jack is not in right now, but if you'd like to leave a message, he'll be happy to return your call when he gets back."

"What are you talking about?"

"I don't know." I laughed. I wanted to scream, but didn't want to appear weak.

"Come over here!" yelled Shakes.

"Can't do it. What for?" I asked.

"Come out of the street!"

I ran down the street until Shakes' voice faded in the distance. I heard music. I ran to the park. It was soothing to hear bands playing in the park. I balanced against a tree. My vision was impaired. I looked up at the tree as the branches beckoned me to come closer. I had a firm grip on the tree and was just about to climb up when Shakes grabbed me.

"What are you doing?" asked Shakes.

"Studying this tree," I said. "The tree of life."

"You're acting like a lunatic and drawing attention to yourself."

"What bands are playing?" I asked.

"Rain, Liquid Sunshine, Evil Farmer, and Electric Blue. I heard that Sublime's going to play tomorrow."

We climbed up the little hill of Anisq'Oyo Park. College kids danced around throwing tortillas in the air. Shakes tried to calm me down. He was a good friend.

"There used to be a joint-rolling contest in the park that brought the community together. There were three joint-rolling contests. One was for the biggest joint, with a two-paper limit. The second was for the best joint rolled. The third was the speed-rolling contest to see who could roll the fastest. The prizes were donated by Bamboo Brothers, a head shop located at on Embarcadero Del Mar. When only a dozen people showed up in 1981, it became obvious that everyone was off snorting coke."

"Let's get out of here," Shakes said.

"The Goldfish-eating Contest starts in a few," I said. "Let's go there."

"It does?" Shakes asked.

"I'm going to write an article on the goldfish contest for the *Nexus*.

"What's your angle on the story?" asked Shakes.

"I entered your name yesterday and put twenty bucks on you."

"You bastard!" he cried.

"This is only the second annual Goldfish-Eating Contest. You've got a pretty good chance of beating out the heavy competition. Especially that Russian foreign exchange student."

"You really think I can do it?" he asked.

"I've got twenty bucks that says you're the man," I said. "The battle consists of three rounds of head-to-head competition. There are going to be some of the ugliest, scariest, most feared freaks in all of Isla Vista drooling all around you. They're going to try and scare you but you're not going to back down."

"I'm not?" he said, looking a little confused.

"Last year's record was eighty-three fish in a minute and forty seconds."

"Eighty-three? That's crazy!"

"Not if you apply physics, my friend. A good mathematical calculation will prove the facts otherwise. I'll explain it on the way."

"Explain to me just one more time why I'm doing this," said Shakes.

"Everybody knows you're a pro-jock. It's time to step up to the challenge and show the whole world what you're made of. Besides, I bet it'll really impress the chicks."

We walked to the pet store. The owner met us out front.

"PETA shut us down!" cried the owner.

"This sucks," I said.

"Let's go home," Shakes said.

My mushroom trip ended. I had clarity. I was thankful to be alive.

CHAPTER 16

When I got home, I found Figgy naked in the bathroom. He was wedged between the bathtub and the toilet. I could tell that he had ingested a bunch of acid and was having a brain surge. His eyes were bloodshot, and every muscle was flexed, like stone. He was shaking and jabbering to himself in a low-pitched drone. I wanted to burst into laughter, but I knew that any sudden move could send him into a deep depression.

"When did you get here?" I asked, calmly.

"Can you see it?" asked Figgy.

"What's that?" I asked.

"The meaning of life," he said.

"You mean, on the shower curtain?" I asked.

"Yes! Can you see it?" asked Figgy.

"Of course," I said, knowing Figgy was having an intensely private experience.

"He can only see the hard skeleton facts and not the fine details," said JC.

"The world is nothing!" Figgy cried.

"You got all that from a shower curtain?" I asked.

"Don't you see?" he asked. "The ego is a social artifact."

"What I see is that you're naked in my bathroom. It's creepy."

"Where do you find these freaks?" asked JC.

"It's college. They just show up."

"He looks like he drank strychnine," said JC, laughing.

"A bitter, poisonous alkaloid to kill vermin?" I asked.

"Yeah," said JC.

"He's so Jell-O-brained that I'm afraid he won't snap out of it."

"Fleeting shadows of an ever-changing life!" screamed Figgy. "Don't you see that it all has to do with the unselfish interest in the welfare of others? There are no answers! Tomorrow is uncertain!" Figgy burst into tears.

JC turned to me with a blank expression. "What a Foolio Iglesias," JC said, shaking his head. "I wish he'd put on some clothes."

"Oh my God!" screamed Figgy.

"Keep it down," I said, putting my finger to my lips. "You're liable to wake the dead."

"Jesus is standing next to you!"

"It's just JC," I said.

"I never believed you," said Figgy. "Can I talk to him?"

"He's a little shy, but give it a try," I said.

"How are you, sir?" shouted Figgy. "It's nice to finally meet you!"

JC was busy going through the medicine cabinet and wasn't paying attention to Figgy. JC had just sprayed on an old bottle of cologne when he realized that Figgy was trying to get his attention. He gave Figgy a look and then disappeared.

"Did I upset him?" asked Figgy.

"JC is like a stealth bomber," I said. "He exists, but you're really not supposed to see him."

"Do you think he likes me?" asked Figgy.

"Of course," I said. "Who wouldn't?"

"How do you know?" asked Figgy.

"Well, he did die for your sins."

"I hope I didn't piss him off."

"Nope," I said. "As soon as we get downtown and he gets a few drinks in him, he'll be as good as new. Are you feeling better now?"

"I feel a bit naked," said Figgy.

"What did you take?" I asked.

"I don't know," said Figgy, "I got here and was waiting for you and I drank some homebrewed beer. Then I just woke up a few seconds ago, and we were talking about something, but I forgot, and I'm feeling warped."

"A bit bonkers, is more like it," I said. "Don't worry. It'll wear off in a few hours. I had some myself."

"If you don't mind," said Figgy. "I'd like to stay here for a little while longer and study this shower curtain."

"Fine by me," I said. I left to put on my Halloween costume.

"What are you going to be?" asked JC.

"A gunfighter," I said.

"Sweet," said JC.

We jumped in the car and rolled up the windows for a hot box session. JC rolled two joints while I fiddled with the radio. The sound kept going in and out. JC handed me a big Bob Marley joint, and we puffed away like two old bastards at a private smoking club.

"We look like the Village People," complained JC.

"What's that show I used to watch?" I asked.

"*Land of the Lost*?" asked JC. "That was such a stupid show."

"Blasphemy," I said. "That's the best show in the world. You should be so lucky you got to watch it. A lot of kids are forced to watch documentaries on how the spork was invented."

"They used dirt and snot for their stage sets," said JC.

"That was back in the 1970s. You could have waved a shiny piece of tinfoil for five hours on a Saturday morning and kids would have loved it."

"Well, nobody ever knows what the hell you're talking about when you bring up those old shows."

"You do," I said. "What two brothers found Sigmund the Sea Monster and kept him hidden from the whole town?"

"Johnny and Scott Stuart," said JC.

"Sing along with me," I said. "Sigmund the Sea Monster and Johnny and Scott are friends. The finest friends to ever be in the land of around the sea!"

"What a great song," said JC, looking annoyed.

"Now, if I could only fix this damn radio." I hit the radio a few times. Bubbles burst around my head. The acid I took came on strong.

We took State Street all the way so that we could smoke some more chronic and avoid the cops. I parked the car around the corner from the Beach Shack. I was looking for Delilah.

Crazy Eddie shouted my name from across the street. I tried to act like I didn't see him, but it was too late. He rolled over in a wheelchair.

"He's going to ruin our whole night," said JC. "This guy is a big minus."

"He's like a phantom," I said. "He lurks in the shadows and waits to cast gloom over our happiness."

"What's going on, bro?" asked Crazy Eddie.

"I hate that word," said JC.

"Not much, Eddie," I said. "We're just going home."

"No!" he shouted. "You can't!"

"He's not going to put us in the trunk again, is he?" asked JC.

"Do you like my costume?" asked Crazy Eddie.

"What are you supposed to be?" I asked.

"I'm you," said Crazy Eddie. "I've got the Hawaiian shirt, the shoes, the hunting jacket, and the hat. Isn't it great? I'm even handing out your business cards."

"Wow," I said, wondering what kind of drugs he was on.

"This guy is crazy," said JC.

"How's the leg?" I asked.

"Just a flesh wound. The doc gave me morphine. The stuff just makes the pain vanish."

"Too bad he didn't overdose," said JC.

"Are you ready to go?" asked Eddie.

"Go where?" I asked.

"TJ! Mexico, baby! South of the border for some señoritas and beers!"

"I'm really not up to it," I said.

"Don't make me force you to go," he said, laughing.

"This guy isn't going to take no for an answer," said JC. Crazy Eddie was whacked on morphine with a gun in the waist of his pants.

"All we need to do is pick up some Shrinky Dinks," I said.

"Shrinky Dinks?" he asked.

"Yeah, I just love those things," I said.

"Are you nuts?" asked JC. "You're not actually thinking about going with this lunatic, are you?"

"Shhh," I hissed.

"What's with all the whispering?" asked Eddie.

"Nothing," I said. "Just got a sore throat."

"You should have a doctor check that out," he said.

"I was thinking the same thing about you," said JC.

"Can I test this wheelchair out before we embark on our journey?"

"I guess," said Eddie. He stood up.

"I've never been in one before. It's cool."

"Just hurry up," he said. "We've got to get those Shrinky Dinks!"

"Pipe down. I just want to take it for a spin. Test out its velocity. Hop in, JC. Hey, Eddie, what's that?" I said, pointing across the street at nothing.

"What?" he said, turning his head away.

"Ah, late!" yelled JC.

We dashed down the street. Crazy Eddie screamed and fired off a few rounds in the night air.

"That bastard," I said, when we got to the car.

We stopped at 7-Eleven to fill up the ice chest I carried in the car for medicinal purposes. We also needed some snacks.

"I heard if you put a penny in your mouth a breathalyzer won't register," said JC.

"Bullshit," I protested.

"The copper manipulates the oxidation."

"Pennies aren't made out of copper anymore," I said.

"So you get an old penny. You know what I mean?"

"Say you get an old penny. How in the hell are you going to talk to a cop with a penny in your mouth?"

"It was just a thought," said JC.

CHAPTER 17

I woke up on a random couch outside a house. A stray dog licked me. I walked over to Woodstock's pizza, but it was closed. I stumbled over to Freebird's for a burrito. It was closed. Nothing was open when I needed it.

"Why don't you buy a T-shirt?" asked JC, pointing across the street.

I jumped back. "Will you stop sneaking up on me?"

"I can't help it," JC giggled.

"What are you doing up so early?" I asked.

"Just getting a breakfast burrito," said JC.

"How'd you get that?" I asked. "The place is closed."

"This is America," said JC. "I can get whatever I want."

"I don't want a T-shirt," I said.

"Sure you do."

"What for?" I asked.

"History is being made, and you're a witness to it. Don't you want something to pass on to the grandkids? You'll need something to remind you that you were in Isla Vista on Halloween. When you're like, fifty."

"Fine. I'll get one if it shuts you up. Which one do you want?"

"Get that one with Scooby-Doo and the Gang," said JC.

"The one with Shaggy and Scooby smoking bong loads in the back of the Mystery Machine?" I asked.

"Yeah, that's the one. 'I break for bong loads.' What a great show that was."

"It used to traumatize me as a small child, but now I see the pure beauty behind its creation."

"Pure brilliance, if you ask me," said JC. "Fred and Daphne were always on speed."

"Trying to solve a spooky mystery," I added.

"Shaggy and Scooby always had the munchies."

"As a result of the 420 nugs." I laughed.

"And Velma was always on acid."

"Could never find her glasses," I added.

"Scooby Doobie Doo where are you?" asked JC.

"And I would have gotten away with it if it wasn't for you snooping, meddling kids."

I forked over ten bucks for the shirt. A bullhorn boomed overhead like a clap of thunder, sending a piercing vibration through my head. I jerked around and found Shakes on a makeshift stage. I felt like I owed it to him to pay attention. He was a full-blown Marxist now. None of the cops bothered to turn around. They were too busy grubbing on free coffee and doughnuts in front of the foot patrol.

"It's time to act!" Shakes shouted. "Wake up, Isla Vista, and resist! Halloween is a party! Isla Vista is not a criminal zone! We are not criminals and should refuse to be mistreated by the pigs! Do you know that the police have placed bets on who can make the most arrests and write the most tickets? What justice is being served to you, Isla Vista? There is a paid militia walking the beat! There are pigs here! Right now! Look around! They have already beaten one man's head in! Who's next? They're waiting to entrap all of you! Remember that all arrests result in at least one night in jail. And most of the evil and atrocious things are done by the pigs! Denying us respect and consideration! And why is the Los Angeles Police Department here, anyway? Who invited them to our party? They're only here to play their silly ego games on us!

They have the guns and the clubs, and we don't! This is our community! We have been denied our justice! Do not listen to their commands, and do not submit to their arrests!"

"What are we listening to this crap for?" asked JC.

"I thought you wanted to hear it?" I said.

"I'm more into religion than politics," said JC.

"You there!" yelled Shakes.

"Him?" I said, pointing to JC.

"I think he means you," said JC, pointing back at me.

"You there," Shakes repeated, pointing directly at me. "Will you join our march?"

"No, thanks," I said. "It sounds exhausting."

"When will you have the time to prevent the pigs from taking over your town?"

"Most likely never," I said. "The Boomers ruined it for me."

"There was already a march to protest this oppressive force that has taken violent control of our community. Yesterday the pigs beat down protesters who came near the barricades. One man was seriously bludgeoned, while the others managed to escape."

"That's great," I said.

"They have beaten some of us!"

"Let's scoop out his brains, and take them to class for examination," said JC.

"Who are you talking to?" Shakes demanded.

"None of your damn business!" shouted JC.

"No one," I said.

"You're crazy!" Shakes hollered.

I shook my head and walked away.

We went over to Isla Vista Market. I bought a super-sized Mountain Dew with lots of ice. JC and I sat in front of the market. Shakes ran over and handed me a three-by-three orange card. He darted off. JC grabbed it and recited it as we walked home.

"If you are stopped by the police," said JC, "you have rights. You can protect these rights if you use this information. You do not have to answer any questions other than your name and address. The police may frisk you for weapons by patting the outside of your clothing. You must not resist arrest, even if you are innocent. As soon as you have been booked, you have the right to complete phone calls to an attorney. The police must give you a receipt for everything taken from you, including your wallet and clothing. You must be allowed to post bail in most cases, but you must be able to post an amount in cash or pay the bail bondsman's fee. The police must bring you into court or release you within forty-eight hours after your arrest, excluding Sundays and holidays. If you do not have money to hire an attorney, immediately ask the police to get you an attorney without charge."

"That's a lot of shit to remember," I said.

"Just don't get arrested," said JC. JC and I walked home and knocked back a few beers.

A few hours later, Crazy Eddie interrupted our peaceful day. "You owe me sixty bucks," Crazy Eddie said, standing in the doorway with a stupid grin on his face.

"What for?" I asked.

"For the keg," he said.

"What keg?" I asked.

"The one you're chipping sixty bucks in for today."

"When did I ever say that?" I asked.

"It was right before you stole my wheelchair," he said.

"Is that how I got all these scratches?" I asked.

"There's no way around it," said JC. "You must pay the fine for drunken, random promises."

It was back to the bank machine, where I'd taken out enough money that weekend to finance a small country. I didn't want to drive my car. It had caused me far too much trouble already. But I had to drive because I was naturally a nice person. I was such a nice person that I ended up putting in eighty bucks for a Fosters keg. Crazy Eddie didn't bring enough money with him to cover the ice and cups.

"I've got a deal for you," said the Crazy Eddie.

"I don't want to hear it," I said, rolling my eyes.

"Why not?" he asked.

"You always have a scheme," I said.

"Just hear me out," he said. "I'll pay you a grand."

"A grand for what?" I asked.

"To crash into my car," he said.

"With my head? Crash into your car?"

"It's more like a dent. You crash into my car, and then I'll get an estimate. I'll get the highest estimate and go to the lowest bidder to fix it. Then I'll pay you a grand, and I'll make money too."

"That's great," I said.

"Are you serious?" he asked.

"Yeah, I didn't think anything was going to make me laugh today. Are you nuts? That's the dumbest idea you've come up with yet. I actually take offense that you'd ask me that."

"Why?" he asked.

"My insurance would go up, dumbass. I'd end up losing money."

"I had to ask," he said.

"No, you didn't have to ask, but you did. You wouldn't be you unless you asked me a question like that. At least you didn't bring up another one of your alien conspiracy theories."

"Why is it that you always lose a sock when you put them in the dryer?"

"This sounds like a real scientific breakthrough," I said.

"The aliens need the socks for their spacecrafts. It's fuel."

"Wow!" I said. "What an incredible discovery."

"It's a proven fact. I've got documentation," he said.

"Then it must be true," I said.

"Can we make a quick stop before we go back to the house?" he asked.

"There's no such thing as a quick stop with you," I said.

"It's a party over on Trigo."

"You always lag hardcore," I said.

"I just need to talk with this dude for two minutes."

"Bullshit," I said. "You'll be inside for an hour while I'm stuck outside."

"Two minutes," he begged. "That's all I ask."

"Nope. I just blew eighty bucks on this keg. I'm going to plant myself next to it all night long. This is it for me. I'm going clean after today."

"There's a keg at this party?" he said.

"Let's go," I said.

I took a quick left and then a right onto Trigo.

"I knew you'd see things my way," said Crazy Eddie.

"Let's get something straight," I said, pulling the car up in front of the party. "I never see things your way. You need help. And I'm not talking about the help you get from those late-night commercials with washed up actors trying to sell you bathing supplies. You need to be put in a cage and poked with a stick—subjected to all kinds of tests so women can wear animal-free makeup and not feel so bad. You've got two minutes."

"Here," he said, placing a hit of X on the dash. "Take this and I'll meet you inside."

"I'll be over by the keg," I said.

I could tell by the unpleasant faces that I wasn't exactly wanted. I didn't feel out of place, but I knew my appearance was odd to them. I was wearing my usual Reyn Spooner shirt, khaki shorts, and green Converse. Everyone else was wearing black leather.

I made my way through the mosh pit to the keg. It stood like a lonely cold soldier in a corner of the front yard. I filled up a cup of beer and leaned against a rickety wooden fence. A punk band played.

"The band scares me," said JC.

"Possible devil worshippers," I added. The sound faded out in a distorted fashion and stopped until the bass player whacked the amp with a rubber mallet.

"I'm not a specialist in music," yelled JC, "but I know crap when I hear it, and this is crap."

"The mosh pit is the only thing keeping me slightly amused," I said.

"I don't see the joy in bashing yourself into someone's chest as hard as you can while keeping a smile on your face."

"It's a legal form of cockfighting," I said.

A guy with a green mohawk climbed up on the roof and jumped into the crowd. The crowd let out a cheer and then a gasp when he landed on the backs of five mosh pitters. Green-haired Boy was so stoked about his newly discovered talent that he climbed right back up on the roof. All the people in the mosh pit thought they'd seen the last of him, but they were wrong. He let out a drunken groan and jumped. The mosh pit parted. Green-haired Boy hit the ground hard. The mosh pit stopped for a moment. Someone grabbed him by his choke collar and dragged him inside.

"Did you see that?" asked JC, filling up a cup at the keg.

"I couldn't have missed it," I said.

"And you didn't even want to come to this party," laughed JC.

"If you go to a party hoping to have a wonderful time, you're doomed. If you go with a shitty attitude and complain the whole way, all you can do is have fun. There's no other way for you to go but up."

"It's very biblical," said JC.

"It's a fact. I've got to find Crazy Eddie and get outta here."

"I thought you were having fun?"

"Are you kidding? This place is kooky."

I found Crazy Eddie sitting on a couch inside the house. Green-haired Boy was curled up in a ball on the floor, moaning. No one thought about calling an ambulance.

"Train's leaving," I said to Crazy Eddie.

"Do you want to get some shrooms?" he asked.

"I guess?" I said, biting my lip. I had forgotten for a moment whose presence I was in. I knew that trying to score would be a long, drawn-out process. However, shrooms sounded mighty good. I didn't want to argue with the idiot in front of a bunch of stoners. One slip of the tongue, and I could be accused of being a Fed.

"You've got to go to the bank, anyway," he said.

"How do you know?" I asked suspiciously.

"You spent all your money on the keg."

"Whatever. Let's just go," I said.

I parked in the red zone in front of the Bank of America ATM, and we all jumped out. There was only one functioning ATM in Isla Vista. I took my place in an endless line for the money monster. I inched forward every few minutes. I finally made it to the front and felt momentarily rich.

"Don't turn around," said JC. The cops are across the street waiting for us."

"They're following me?"

"Let them tow the thing," said JC.

"I'm not going through that nightmare again."

I could feel the adrenaline pumping. I walked swiftly to my car. I figured I could get a good hundred yards ahead of them, take a quick left, and dump the car. If I had to, I'd make a run for the UCSB campus.

"Here they come," said JC.

"I can't go left!" I moaned. "I can't go right either, or go any other direction, because of all these people. Where did they come from?"

I was stuck. I prayed for an earthquake. A giant sinkhole. A hurricane, tornado, cyclone, tidal wave, stampede. Something. Any natural disaster would do.

I searched my car for a breath mint. I pulled over in front of Pot Stickers and thought about getting myself some egg rolls. I scrambled for my wallet and all the necessary paperwork.

"Perhaps a bribe?" suggested JC.

"What's going on back there?" I asked.

JC replied in a British accent, "The Sheriff of Nottingham is writing in his little black book with one foot on the bumper of his cruiser."

"He must be waiting for backup."

"A wanted felon," said JC.

The cop came to the window.

"Here's my license, sir. Is there a problem? Did I do something wrong? Was I speeding? Did I not signal at that last turn? Are all my tags in order?"

"Is he ignoring you?" asked JC.

The cop lifted the windshield wiper.

"He's going to rip off every part of the car," I whispered.

The cop slapped a ticket on the window and walked away. I reached out the window and grabbed the ticket.

"What does it say?" asked JC.

"It's a ticket for parking in a red zone," I said.

The cop drove off. I got out. I left the car unlocked, hoping it would get stolen.

"Where the hell have you been?" shouted Crazy Eddie. "I've been waiting forever."

"I hate you."

"What the hell, man? I've got things to do. I don't have time to wait around."

"You might as well punch him now," said JC.

I couldn't punch Crazy Eddie. After all, he was a friend. I walked home. I got ready for Halloween. I dressed up in my costume. I was a Sheriff. I put on brown polyester pants and a brown cotton shirt. I added handcuffs, pepper spray, rubber baton, toy cap gun.

"What's the first aid kit for?" asked JC.

"Just in case I have to resuscitate someone," I said.

I put on my dark blue cap that said "NARCOTICS OFFICER" and stepped out into the backyard, where a party raged. The Fosters keg was put to good use. The crowd parted when everyone saw me. A few people jumped the fence as I made my way to a group standing next to the keg.

"Damn!" said Shakes, grabbing his heart. "You scared the shit out of me!"

"How do you like it?" I asked.

"It's cool," he said. "Some girl named Delilah called for you."

"Did she say where she is?" I asked excitedly.

"She's at the Trop Dorms and wants you to stop by."

"Can I borrow your bike?" I asked.

"Just lock it up. It's my fifth bike this quarter."

"Well, it wouldn't be Isla Vista if you didn't get your bike stolen."

"That's true," said Shakes.

"I think all the bike shops are just fronts for the mob," said JC.

I made my way over to the liquor store and picked up a bottle of vodka. I had problems getting in the dorm because of security. I went around back to try my luck there.

I was met by a disturbed R.A. The resident advisors were the easiest ones to spot, because they were the only sober-looking people in Isla Vista.

"Can I help you?" she growled.

"I'm looking for a girl," I said.

"What room is she in?" she demanded.

"That's a good question," I said.

"Do you live here?" the R.A. inquired.

"No way, this place is for losers. I lived here as a freshman, but I didn't know any better."

"No visitors until Monday," she said.

"I just need to talk to her really quick," I said.

"Is that alcohol you have there?" she asked, pointing to the bottle of vodka that I'd neglected to hide.

"Yes, it is. My friend. She's a diabetic and needs this to calm her nerves. It's all perfectly legal. Ask anyone."

"You can't bring liquor in here," she said.

"I'll leave it outside."

"What you're doing is against the law," she said.

"What is?" I asked.

"It's called an 'open container.' "

I shoved the bottle into her hands. "Hey, you can't bring that in here!" I shouted.

"What?"

"That's alcohol! She's got liquor in her hands everybody!" I yelled.

"Be quiet," she hissed.

"I'm calling the cops on you!" I shouted.

I rode off.

CHAPTER 18

Isla Vista hadn't seen so many cops since William Kunstler spoke to a crowd of four thousand on February 25, 1970. The day before, local activists had been arrested, and two hundred people had gathered at the Loop to throw rocks, set trash cans on fire, and vandalize buildings.

Following his speech, the cops patrolled Isla Vista with an iron fist. The cops stumbled upon a student with a bottle of wine and arrested him for possession of a Molotov cocktail. Later that night, police cars were set on fire and the Bank of America building was burned. The first Isla Vista riot went on for several days until Governor Reagan called in the National Guard.

In early April, Jerry Rubin was prohibited from speaking in Santa Barbara County. Campus radio was shut down for violating federal law.

Kevin Moran was shot and killed by a Santa Barbara policeman who claimed the shot was fired by an imaginary sniper. The police took no responsibility. A court inquiry ruled the death accidental. A plaque was placed on a sidewalk in Isla Vista in memory of Kevin. Kevin Moran was just a kid from Santa Clara County.

Indictments were handed down in June to those who burned the bank to the ground. The *Santa Barbara 17* was a list of the most outspoken and effective political leaders in town. Two of the seventeen had been in jail the night the bank burned. The trial was set for the summer when most of the students would be out of town. Four hundred people were arrested at the sit-in, at Perfect Park. The Los Angeles Tactical Squad was brought in to enforce curfew and tear-gassing students.

The result of the ordeal was more than three hundred signed complaints against law enforcement officers, alleging that one hundred thirteen people were beaten, sixty dwellings were illegally entered and searched, forty-eight instances of willful destruction of personal property occurred, and thirty-four people were apprehended on private property for curfew violations.

Everyone at the house was drunk when I got back. Halloween had begun. I was in my Sheriff's costume.

JC and I hit the streets. We had to take a detour because a black cat crossed our path. We just didn't want bad magic vibes. It was a bad omen waiting to happen. We passed a billboard.

HAVE A GOOD HALLOWEEN, BUT REMEMBER:

1. BUYING ALCOHOL FOR A MINOR IS ILLEGAL AND WILL RESULT IN A NIGHT IN JAIL PLUS FINES.

2. VIOLATING THE COUNTY ORDINANCE PROHIBITING LOUD MUSIC DURING THE EVENING AND FOLLOWING MORNING FROM 6 P.M. TO 7 A.M. FROM OCTOBER 28 TO NOVEMBER 1 IS A MISDEMEANOR.

3. CARRYING OPEN CONTAINERS OF ALCOHOL AND DRINKING IN PUBLIC WILL RESULT IN A $100 FINE FOR THE FIRST OFFENSE, $200

FOR THE SECOND OFFENSE, AND $500 FOR THE THIRD OFFENSE WITHIN A VIOLATION YEAR.

4. A MINOR IN POSSESSION WILL MEAN A FINE OF $108 AND DRIVER'S LICENSE SUSPENSION FOR ONE YEAR.

5. DRIVING UNDER THE INFLUENCE WILL RESULT IN A MINIMUM $1300 FINE PLUS DRIVER'S LICENSE SUSPENSION FOR A YEAR AND THREE YEARS PROBATION FOR OFFENDERS UNDER THE AGE OF 21.

6. MOST MISDEMEANORS, SUCH AS PUBLIC INTOXICATION, AS WELL AS FELONIES WILL MEAN AT LEAST A NIGHT IN COUNTY JAIL PLUS FINES AND COURT COSTS.

7. ANYONE UNDER 21 YEARS OF AGE WHO IS STOPPED FOR ANY REASON AND WHOM THE OFFICER SUSPECTS OF ALCOHOL CONSUMPTION WILL BE ADMINISTERED A TEST ON THE SPOT, AND ANY MEASURABLE AMOUNT OF ALCOHOL WILL RESULT IN IMMEDIATE LOSS OF DRIVER'S LICENSE.

8. TAKE CARE OF EACH OTHER, ESPECIALLY FRIENDS WHO HAVE HAD TOO MUCH TO DRINK, AND TREAT EACH OTHER WITH RESPECT.

9. STAY AWAY FROM THE CLIFFS!

P.S. HAVE A NICE DAY.

We walked through a few houses and hooked back around until we were heading toward the cliffs. We were two blocks away from Del Playa. I heard a voice call after me.

"Stop!"

"Just keep walking," said JC.

"Maybe if we pretend we didn't hear him, he won't chase after us."

"Too late now," said JC. "Here comes the clatter of a galloping horse."

It was a deputy on horseback. "I'm taking your costume," the deputy yelled.

"It's a costume. I've worn it three years in a row. No one's ever hassled me about it before."

"This year it's different," said the deputy.

"It's politics," said JC.

"You'd better come with me and talk to my sergeant."

I followed the deputy to the command post a few blocks down. He took me to his sergeant. A line of drunks sat on a bench waiting to be transported to the county jail.

"Hey, Sarge, look what I found," said the deputy.

The sergeant looked me up and down.

"It's a nice costume," laughed the sergeant.

"What should we do with him?" the deputy asked.

"Let him go."

"Why?"

"It's a costume. It's Halloween. It's Isla Vista."

"But it's a crime to impersonate an officer."

"He's not impersonating anyone. It's a costume."

A bunch of cops gathered around to gawk at me. Shakes appeared and screamed at the top of his lungs.

"You pigs!" Shakes screamed. "How can you do this! Taking innocent, defenseless puppies and turning them into killing machines. Such gentle creatures. Those poor animals!

You do it for your own sick pleasure! You are fucking murderers!"

"Someone shut him up!" a cop yelled.

The cops arrested Shakes for disturbing the peace.

"That's one hell of a costume," said another cop. "They're going to like you in the fun house, pretty boy!"

"You can pick up your costume on Monday at the foot patrol," the deputy said.

"Don't fall for that trap," said JC. "They'll arrest you the second you walk in."

I began to walk off but the deputy on horseback came up beside me and tried to be my buddy.

"I'm sorry about that whole thing," he said.

"This is the same bastard who tried to arrest you," said JC.

"You were just doing your job," I said, trying to brush him off.

"You don't want to be dressed up like us," he said.

"It was just a costume. It's Halloween."

"I'm out here every day and it gets crazy."

"Thanks, and have a good night," I said.

I nodded and walked down the street.

"What an asshole," said JC.

"That would be a good choice of words," I said.

"They're so annoying."

"He just wanted to be cool," I said.

"Why do cops have to always kick down the philosophy when they know they're wrong?"

"It makes 'em feel better," I said. "They think they have to make a difference in your life."

"Like anyone cares."

"You've got to know when to hold 'em and when to fold 'em."

"Kenny Rogers knows."

"I'm going home. I've had it with this place. I don't think I've slept in four days. I'm exhausted."

"Quitter," said JC.

"That's me."

"You can't give up now. We were just getting started. Things were just getting interesting."

"You try getting harassed by the cops. Then tell me how interesting it is."

"You're a nonconformist," said JC.

I had an epiphany. The gears shifted. I needed to find Delilah. I needed to get sober. I needed to get my life in order. I needed to grow up. I needed to find Delilah.

I ran to Del Playa.

I strolled by the Halfway House, the Disco Hut, the Big Yellow House, and the Bob Marley House. Every house seemed to have a name in Isla Vista. I saw Cheech and Chong; keystone cops; Richard Nixon and all the other American presidents; Karl Marx; Bastard Boy (don't ask); a giant bong; Desert Storm commandos; The Little Rascals; Freud; Mozart; Fatty Arbuckle; Elvis; Gumby and Pokey; the whole *Star Wars* crew; Sid and Nancy; Mighty Mouse; the Knights of the Round Table; Caesar; Queen Elizabeth; Rocky and Rambo; clowns; mimes; ghosts; the Peanuts gang; The Little Rascals again; pimps; hookers; used car salesmen; gangsters; mobsters; hippies; zoo animals; and the Legion of Doom. Halloween had exploded before my eyes.

I was on the 6500 block when I heard someone call my name. It was Delilah. She was dressed like a scarecrow with hay coming out of her arms, and neck. She was a vision.

"I've been looking all over for you," said Delilah.

"I've been looking for you too," I smiled.

She threw her arms around me. "We're throwing a party right here. Come with me."

"I'll never leave you."

"I've been waiting to tell you something ever since the other night."

"What's that?" I asked.

Before she could say another word, she keeled over and face-planted to the ground. The cops saw Delilah fall and rushed over.

"She's with me," I said. "Get up, sweetheart. The cops are right there." I picked her up and carried her into the party. I set her down on the couch.

A brunette dressed as a cheerleader bent down and touched Delilah's face. "Is she going to be all right?" the cheerleader asked.

"She's just drunk," I said.

"I know you," the cheerleader said. "You're that writer. You were in one of my classes. I think you attacked the professor."

"He had it coming," I said.

"I liked your book," she said. "It was very sumptuous."

"Most people just say it sucks," I said.

She introduced me to the doctor, who stood next to a guy dressed as roadkill.

"Do you want some acid?" asked the doctor.

"You've got to be joking? It's almost two in the morning."

"I've got a whole bunch of it. It's free."

"Hell, if it's free," I said, "hand it over." The last thing I wanted was to fry my balls off. I was already going out of my mind, but I couldn't pass up free acid.

"It's washout acid, but it's just the same," he explained, handing me three 5x7 sheets of wax paper from his pocket.

"Washout?" I asked.

"Yeah, it's just the stuff I mopped up when I made a fresh batch of acid. Try it."

I licked the wax paper. It zapped my tongue. "It's electric all right," I smiled.

"It's great stuff," said the doctor.

"Here," I said. "Have some surgical gloves."

"What are you doing with surgical gloves?" he asked, looking at me strangely.

"A lot of people carry them around. You can never be too safe these days."

"He's right, ya know," said the cheerleader.

"Never thought about it that way before," said the doctor.

"Well, you should," I said. "Just because you're a doctor doesn't mean you know everything."

A downpour of thoughts invaded my head like they were being displayed on giant billboards. My flesh felt like it was melting, but in a good way. I knew that I was beginning to peak heavily. When you're on chemicals, it is possible to conceive the self as being only partially involved in the immediate action around you. You're there, but you aren't there. You can be standing right next to someone, and yet they are a million miles away. Items are dropped and added, weakening sectors of what is still being taken for granted.

Words paraded around me: trauma—shock—the number 15—re-examination—distort—Speed up—slow down—problematics of time—Constructs of reality—Blink—Think—Look—Really pay attention in class next quarter—William Holden and Sunset Boulevard—Life-Death—Land of the Lost—delusions—ambiguous—fickle—Vanity—placebos—liberation—Cindy Crawford—rigorous—Green Lantern—Altruism—I'm dying—ice water—urged—Tom Watson—omnipotent—agony—Space 1999—the Lakers—Chevy Chase—Bonanza—Dominatrix—sabotage—Adam Sandler—funny—ice hockey—Count Chocula cereal—I feel so alive—lush—Ted Kennedy—From the edge—Who isn't random in this godforsaken place?

It was all rolled up into a blazing fireball. A thousand track switches clicked in sequence. I became a transparent eyeball. I could see everything. A massless particle. I was rich in illuminating insights that only made sense to me.

I spotted Figgy across the room. I could tell that he knew exactly what I was thinking. Galactic telepathy. I moved toward him.

"I think I'm dying," Figgy said.

"Do you want some acid?" I asked.

"Is it blotter or micro dot?" he asked.

"Neither. It's just a bunch of purple and orange spots on wax paper."

"Give it to me," he said.

I took out two sheets and handed them to him. Figgy gobbled down the two sheets of acid like a wild dog. "Got any more?" he asked.

"You're joking?"

From the look on his face, I knew he was dead serious.

"Give it to me," he demanded with a slight rage in his voice.

I handed over the last sheet, and he gobbled it down.

"Are you satisfied?" I asked.

"Very," he said.

"That's the most acid I've ever seen anyone take in my entire life." I wondered how long Figgy was going to trip. Would he fry for a year, or the rest of his life? Only time would tell.

"I was just talking to JC," said Figgy.

"Really? What did he say?" I asked.

"He didn't say much."

"Did he say anything at all?" I asked. "Like some Bible quotes?"

"Not really," Figgy said.

"What was he wearing?" I asked.

"Clothing."

I looked over at JC. "That's what he looks like," I said, not wanting to upset Figgy's trip.

"I knew I'd seen him," said Figgy.

"He's very popular," I added. I filled a cookie jar with beer and made my way to the front of the house. A few people loomed around the front yard fence. I climbed up to the makeshift deck and sat on a tree stump between Santa Claus and the Creature from the Black Lagoon. The crowds were thin. The cops were making their rounds trying to get everyone to go home. I was amused listening to Santa yell at people passing by.

"Hey, fruitcake!" screamed Santa. "Nice costume! What the fuck are you supposed to be? Look at this guy right here! Oh, it's a security guard! The big man on the streets! He doesn't have a gun, but he's got his clipboard!" The crowd erupted with laughter. I choked on a mouthful of beer.

"You shouldn't have fucked with security," said the Creature from the Black Lagoon.

"Oh, why the fuck not? I'm Santa Claus!"

"Here come the cops!"

"Oh, shit!" cried Santa.

The cops rushed the fence knocking us down. I hit the ground hard.

"Do you live here?" a cop demanded.

"No," I said.

"Then get the fuck out of here and go home," he growled.

"Sure thing."

The cops were sweeping the streets on horseback. I walked to the right, but the cops wouldn't let me go by.

"Can't go this way," one of the cops yelled at me.

"Which way can I go?" I asked.

"Not this way," yelled another cop.

I walked into a wall of cops on horseback. I thought I would be trampled to death.

"Can't go this way," yelled another cop.

"What do you want me to do?" I asked. "I can't go left, and I can't go right."

"I don't care," said the cop. "Just get the hell out of here." The cops had me surrounded. Two cops ran toward me. I took off toward the cliffs.

"Up here!" shouted JC, standing on the balcony of an apartment.

"I see ya," I said, running toward him.

I jumped up on a car and took a flying leap to catch a balcony railing. I used all my strength to pull myself up. I collapsed on the balcony. The cops turned around.

"Click your heels twice, and you'll be home in no time," said JC. We waited until the streets were empty. I looked out over Del Playa.

"Halloween weekend is over," I said.

"Who won? Who lost?" asked JC.

"Who cares?" I said. "You move on. You don't dwell. It's college and you learn not to ask any questions. The randomness just goes on."

A heavy fog rolled in. The streets were empty. It was peacefully quiet. I climbed down from the balcony and made my way back to the party. Delilah was gone. I wandered through the house and found Figgy huddled in a corner of the kitchen, arranging matchsticks on the floor.

"Are you okay?" I asked.

"The cops were here, and then I sat down, and then everyone was gone, and then I found these matches, and I figured out a new mathematical formula."

"That's great," I said. "I was thinking about going home now."

"Please don't leave me alone," Figgy pleaded.

"Why not?" I asked.

"I can't remember where I live," said Figgy.

"That's all right. We're in Isla Vista."

"I don't know who you are," said Figgy, "but could you please take me home?"

"Don't worry," I said. "I'll take you home. You're staying at my house."

I took Figgy home, then left to find Delilah. I lit a cigarette and walked to the cliffs.

"Poor guy," said JC. "Doesn't even know where he lives."

"Drugs will do that to you," I said.

"You were put here to help him," said JC. "Just for a moment. It's all we have on earth. Little moments." JC motioned me to follow him. We got to Del Playa. He handed me a cold soldier. Everything seemed so perfect. Mornings like these made me understand my existence.

"What's the purpose of life?" I asked JC.

"You're about to find out."

Delilah approached on a beach cruiser. "I've been looking all over for you," she said.

"Me too." I smiled.

"I've been meaning to ask you … Do you want to move to Hollywood with me? I thought maybe you could write the great American novel."

"Yes."

"What I'm trying to say is, I love you."

"I love you too."

"You do?"

"I always have. Since the first moment I saw you."

"Do you want to watch the sunrise with me at Campus Point?"

"Yes."

"I've got to go," said JC.

"What do you mean?" I asked.

"Our time is up."

"Delilah, can you give me a moment?" I asked. "This is going to sound insane, but I need to talk to Jesus. If that scares you, I understand. I know it sounds strange."

"This is Isla Vista," she said. "Nothing sounds strange."

I took a few steps back. "Where are you going?" I asked JC.

"Sorry buddy, but this is the end of the line."

"Why?"

"It's time to let you go. It's been fun, but it's just creepy now. I've been here for too long. We had a good run."

"But I don't want to be alone."

"You won't be. You have Delilah. You asked me what the purpose of life is. It's Delilah. It's love. The purpose of life is love. It pushes us to be better. My job was to bring you two together."

"So why didn't you just say that from the start?"

"It doesn't work that way. Follow her. She will lead you to a better life. Love drives us."

"Aren't you going to leave me with a proverb or something?"

"What do you want?"

"I don't know. Something profound maybe."

"Everything works out in the end, or it doesn't." JC vanished.

I turned to Delilah. She grabbed my hand. We kissed. It was electric. It was everything I always wanted. It was Isla Vista.

ABOUT THE AUTHOR

Mike Knox is a writer, epilepsy advocate, and stand-up comedian who has performed at The Comedy Store, the Hollywood Improv, and the Pasadena Ice House. A former corrections officer at California State Prison, Los Angeles County, and a retired parole agent for the California Department of Corrections and Rehabilitation, he lives in Valencia, California, with his wife and daughter; for the gift of their love, he feels both lucky and unworthy. He can be seen on the hit TV series *Elkhorn*, playing the town drunkard. He is the author of three books.

ABOUT THE PUBLISHER

The Sager Group was founded in 1984. In 2012 it was chartered as a multimedia content brand, with the intent of empowering those who create art—an umbrella beneath which makers can pursue, and profit from, their craft directly, without gatekeepers. TSG publishes books; ministers to artists and provides modest grants; and produces documentary, feature, and commercial films. By harnessing the means of production, The Sager Group helps artists help themselves. For more information, please see www.TheSagerGroup.net.

MORE FROM
THE SAGER GROUP

The Swamp: Deceit and Corruption in the CIA
An Elizabeth Petrov Thriller (Book 1)
by Jeff Grant

Eat Wheaties: A Novel
by Michael Kun

#MeAsWell: A Novel
by Peter Mehlman

Death Came Swiftly: Novel About the Tay Bridge Disaster of 1879
by Bill Abrams

High Tolerance: A Novel of Sex, Race, Celebrity, Murder ... and Marijuana
by Mike Sager

Miss Havilland: A Novel
by Gay Daly

The Orphan's Daughter: A Novel
by Jan Cherubin

Lifeboat No. 8: Surviving the Titanic
by Elizabeth Kaye

Into the River of Angels: A Novel
by George R. Wolfe

Goodbye, Sweetberry Park: A Novel of City Life,
Creeping Gentrification and Flesh-eating Snakes
by Josh Green

See our entire library at TheSagerGroup.net

THE SAGER GROUP
Artifex Te Adiuva